GEEKS, GIRLS, AND SECRET IDENTITIES

BY
MIKE JUNG

WITH ILLUSTRATIONS BY
MIKE MAIHACK

ARTHUR A. LEVINE BOOKS
AN IMPRINT OF SCHOLASTIC INC.

Library of Congress Cataloging-in-Publication Data

Jung, Mike.
Geeks, girls, and secret identities / by Mike Jung ; with illustrations by
Mike Maihack. — 1st ed.   p. cm.
Summary: Twelve-year-old Vincent and his fellow members of the Captain Stupendous Fan
Club help out when someone new becomes Earth's most famous superhero, without knowing
anything about him, just as evil Professor Mayhem and his robot arrive in Copperplate City.

ISBN 978-0-545-33548-5 (hardcover : alk. paper) [1. Superheroes—Fiction. 2. Clubs—
Fiction. 3. Robots—Fiction. 4. Middle schools—Fiction. 5. Schools—Fiction. 6. Humorous stories.
7. Science fiction.] I. Maihack, Mike, ill. II. Title.
PZ7.J953Gee 2012 [Fic] —dc23
                                                                2011042548

10 9 8 7 6 5 4 3 2 1   12 13 14 15 16

Printed in the U.S.A. 23

First edition, October 2012

FOR MIRANDA, ZOE, AND LEO

CHAPTER

There are four Captain Stupendous fan clubs in Copperplate City, but ours is the only one that doesn't suck. There's the Official Captain Stupendous Fan Club (they hold a trademark on the name, including "Official"), the Friends of Stupendous (a group of rich old ladies, if you can believe it), the Stupendites (a bunch of girls who probably spend all their time trying on each other's clothes), and us. We're the Captain Stupendous Fan Club, period. We're the real deal, even if we are the smallest fan club in the city. Maybe in the country. Possibly on the entire planet.

So when a giant robot came to town and picked a fight right outside Spud's Pizza, you can guess how psyched I was. Everyone who's ever lived in Copperplate City has seen at least one Stupendous battle in person, but it never gets old. And Spud's is in my neighborhood!

I was there with my best friends, George and Max, the other two-thirds of the fan club. Sadly, so were all forty billion members of the Official Captain Stupendous Fan Club, hogging the middle of the restaurant with their oh-we're-so-great-and-you're-not attitude. That's the problem with hanging out at Spud's on Saturday—everyone else is there too. George, Max, and I were at our usual table next to the recycling bins. George was across from me, and Max and I were facing the front door.

Max socked me on the arm and pointed over George's shoulder. "Hey, Vincent, isn't that your girlfriend?"

I looked up, then jerked my eyes down to the table.

Polly Winnicott-Lee from school! Holy banana! She was with some friend who jabbered away like a human machine gun. Oh dude, they were sitting down right behind George!

"She's not my girlfriend," I said.

"You are SO in love with her, dude," Max said. "You should just accept it."

George turned around, and I threw a crumpled napkin at him.

"Don't look!" I said.

"You loooooooooove her," George said in a really high voice.

"Shut up," I said. I grabbed a slice and took a huge chomp out of it. A little bit of sauce oozed from the corner of my mouth.

"Eating like you were raised by a family of gorillas isn't gonna impress her, you know," Max said.

I opened my pizza-filled mouth and showed it to Max.

"She just saw you do that," he said, cackling.

I swallowed. "You think so?" I took a quick peek, but Polly wasn't looking at all. I licked my thumb and pretended to stab it into Max's pizza.

"You think she's a Captain Stupendous fan?" Max asked. He shook a bunch of red pepper onto a slice of pepperoni.

"NO," George said. "She's a GIRL."

"Oh little dude, you have so much to learn." Max shook his head slowly. "Girls are not the enemy."

"The Stupendites are girls," I said.

"The Stupendites are like those dinosaurs with the long necks, they have brains the size of walnuts," George said. "And, Max, you know I'm taller than you, right?" He shook some salt onto a pizza crust and stuffed the whole thing in his mouth.

"Take Stacy Park, for example," Max said.

"Yeah, yeah, Stacy Park, whatever," George said.

"Stacy Park's in high school, dude." Max put a hand

on George's shoulder. "And you saw her in that bikini at McQueen Beach, just like I did."

"When did you guys go to the beach?" I said. "And where was I?"

"I don't know, maybe you were hanging out with your girlfriend." Max grinned, which made big creases on either side of his mouth, then stuck out his tongue. The stuck-out tongue combined with the bristliness of his brown hair made him look like a round-headed German Shepherd.

Every cell phone in the place started ringing at once, which could only mean one thing. I dug my phone out of my pocket, and sure enough, a text from the Copperplate City alert system.

STUPENDOUS ALERT: GIANT ROBOT. 24TH & BYRNE.

"Stupendous Alert!" I yelled. Okay, a bunch of other kids yelled it too, but I yelled it first, even if nobody heard me.

"That's right around the corner!" George said.

There was a crackly sound from the ceiling, then a voice.

"Attention, Spud's customers, we are on Stupendous Alert. Please stay in your seats. DON'T GO OUTSIDE. Again, we are on Stupendous Alert. DO NOT GO OUTSIDE."

"Let's go outside!" one of the Official Fan Club guys shouted.

Two seconds later a huge *BOOM* shook the building.

Dishes rattled, pizza crust hit the floor, and the littler kids in the room started crying.

One of the "Officials" stood on a table and waved his fist at the ceiling. It was Scott Fanelli, who went to our school and was the thorn in the side of my life. "Go get 'em, Captain!" he yelled. His obnoxious buddies cheered, and I saw Polly look over and roll her eyes.

BOOM! POW! CRASH!

"Look!" George shouted, pointing at the windows on the other side of the pizza parlor. A metal foot the size of a fire truck crashed down outside, completely blocking our view of the Chinese restaurant across the street.

"We're going outside!" It was Scott, being a big show-off. The Officials cheered again and stampeded for the door. The intercom voice kept saying, "DO NOT GO OUTSIDE. . . . SERIOUSLY, DON'T GO. . . ."

"Hey, guys," I said. "You know, I think we should . . ."

"Come ON!" Max said.

There were so many people by the front door that we couldn't even see it, but Max lowered his shoulder and slammed into the crowd like he was scoring a touchdown. George looked at me, cackled, and dove into the crowd after Max.

I shook my head. ". . . maybe go outside. Sure, Vincent, great idea . . ."

I followed George, just barely making it into the gap Max had opened up in the crowd. After a lot of elbows and stepped-on feet we made it outside.

Spud's is on a busy corner, and the intersection was clogged with cars that people had just left in the middle of the street. That's usually a good idea during a battle with a giant villain—nobody wants to get stomped into a human waffle. The grown-ups were crammed into doorways and alleys, but the kids were all over the place, staring up at the sky. The Officials chanted, "STU-PEN-DOUS, STU-PEN-DOUS," pumping their fists on each syllable.

Captain Stupendous in action! There he was, floating over the Chinese restaurant and next to the SuperSuites Hotel, which is thirty floors high. Stupendous was probably twenty floors up. His cape flapped out behind him, and the sun twinkled off the logo on his chest. Half a block away the robot also hovered in midair, although its feet were closer to the ground. It must have been forty or fifty feet tall, with lots of gray metal bolts coming out of the joints, and big clomping feet. It wasn't smooth and rounded with funky spikes, like the robots in Japanese anime. It looked like something from an old movie.

"Dude, that is such a cool robot," George said as he cracked his knuckles. George has these huge knobby knuckles, which make his arms look even skinnier than they are. "It's old-school."

Stupendous laughed. It was amazing how clearly we heard it. It even made the Officials stop their idiotic chant.

"COME ON, YOU OVERGROWN TIN TOY!" Stupendous shouted. "WHOEVER YOU ARE, YOU CAN DO BETTER THAN THAT!"

Max, George, and I looked at each other.

"Are we talking about a *brand-new villain?*" I said. "Do you think—"

"SOON EVERYONE WILL KNOW WHO I AM, CAPTAIN STUPENDOUS!" This time it was the robot talking, and an "Ooooohhhh" went up from the crowd. I swear, people just love clichéd villain talk.

"A NEW VILLAIN!" It was Scott again—this time he was standing on a car.

"YOU FACE PROFESSOR MAYHEM, DOLT!" the robot said.

"Aw, geez, Professor Mayhem, that name sucks," George said.

"Like you'd come up with a better name," Max said, punching George on the shoulder without looking.

"I HOPED FOR AT LEAST A MODICUM OF ENTERTAINMENT DURING MY FIRST ENCOUNTER WITH YOU, STUPENDOUS! YOU DISAPPOINT ME!"

"WELL, LET'S SEE IF I CAN MAKE THINGS A LITTLE MORE ENTERTAINING!" Stupendous shouted, then, *WAZOWIE*, he flew at the robot like a lightning bolt. All the kids raced out of the street. When the real fighting starts it's good to find cover; sometimes stuff comes crashing out of the sky. We ended up crammed into the doorway of an antiques shop with a bunch of other people, including Polly Winnicott-Lee and her friend.

The robot flexed its arms, brought its feet together, and flew straight up. Stupendous didn't change direction at all—he hit the robot's feet, grabbed one with both arms, and flew up and behind the robot, flipping it upside down.

The robot doubled over at the waist and grabbed Stupendous by the legs, which was impressive when you consider how big it was. The thing with any big enemy—whether it's a robot, monster, alien, or genetically altered human—is lack of speed. They're slow, and with his superspeed the Captain usually takes care of business in a hurry. This robot was faster than your typical fifty-foot-tall bad guy.

No biggie, though—Stupendous kicked out hard and knocked the robotic hands off his legs. He accelerated, snapping the robot back out to its full length, then he whipped the whole robot in a big arc and threw it straight up in the air. The robot went into some kind of crazy gymnastic flip, but Stupendous closed the gap between them in an eyeblink and landed a punch right in the middle of the robot's back. The robot's head snapped back and its arms and legs flailed around as it flew even higher into the air.

Everyone on the street burst into cheers. The robot recovered and spun around in midair, but by then Stupendous had already zoomed past it and way up into the atmosphere.

"Meteor Strike!" I yelled.

"METEOR STRIKE!" Scott yelled, just a microsecond after I did.

CLANGGGG! We couldn't see it from underneath, but Stupendous must have come out of the sky like a meteor and slammed into the robot. Its limbs flew straight out from its body as it hurtled down toward the street. Everybody screamed as the robot came crashing down, but Stupendous caught it by one arm, forty or fifty feet up, preventing it from demolishing the street. The robot jerked crazily, kicking its legs.

"A TEN-YEAR-OLD GIRL COULD TAKE YOU DOWN, PROFESSOR MAYPOLE!" Stupendous said.

"THAT'S 'MAYHEM'! 'MAYHEM'!"

"SO SORRY, I MEANT TO SAY 'MAYFLY'!"

"AAAARRRGH!" The robot pulled its arm down hard,

snapping Stupendous like a whip, and its whole torso suddenly spun like a top, turning its arms into a kind of giant, killer helicopter propeller.

WHAMMO! Stupendous got clobbered, and the impact sent him flying back down into the street. He crashed into an abandoned mail truck, which imploded and spit boxes and envelopes all over the cars behind it. One of the truck's doors popped off and came flying in our direction, which made everyone around me (including me) scream like lunatics. Some people ducked or raised their arms, but I just stood there and watched the door of death come at me like a rocket.

At the last possible nanosecond, two sets of fingers appeared at the top and bottom of the door, stopping it in its tracks. The whole bunch of us said, "Aaaahhhhh . . ." all at once as Stupendous flipped the door over his shoulder.

"Everyone all ri—" He stopped in midsentence and stared at somebody for a second. I craned my neck to look in the same direction—it looked like he was staring at Polly! What was that all about?

The robot landed hard, stomping one foot right down on top of Stupendous, maybe two feet in front of us. It felt like the whole street and everything on it bounced into the air—screaming kids, screaming parents, cars, everything. I fell backward, but the person behind me fell forward, so I somehow ended up standing on my feet. Over to the left I saw someone topple forward and land on the robot's foot. It was Polly.

The robot looked down at its foot and launched back into the air, with Polly still hanging on. I heard her screaming as she left the ground.

Stupendous came right up out of the broken concrete and grabbed for the robot's foot, but he missed his grip.

". . ."

Oh man, I really tried to say something. I TRIED. But nothing came out.

"THERE'S A GIRL UP THERE!" Scott just wouldn't shut up! He had his chest stuck out like it was *him* fighting the new villain. Doofus. "ON THE ROBOT'S FOOT! SAVE HER!"

Stupendous's eyes (which you can actually see since he's one of the few heroes who doesn't wear a mask) opened up really wide. He went straight up at the robot's foot, but the robot must have seen him, because it spun completely around, taking out a chunk of the SuperSuites Hotel with one fist. It brought its foot up fast and tipped Polly into its hand—they were already so high up in the air that she was a little hard to see.

Stupendous juked to the right, then to the left, like he was trying to fake the robot out. The robot (dude, it was so fast) didn't go for it, though; it just hung there with Polly cradled in one hand.

"LET HER GO, PROFESSOR!" Stupendous shouted, and the laughing tone was completely gone—he was all business now. "LET HER GO BEFORE YOU GET INTO TROUBLE YOU CAN'T GET OUT OF!"

"STAY BACK, STUPENDOUS!" Professor Mayhem said. "IT APPEARS YOU'RE AS FORMIDABLE AS YOUR REPUTATION WOULD HAVE IT! WELL DONE!"

"RELEASE THE GIRL, PROFESSOR!"

"AS YOU WISH, *MON CAPITAINE*! YOU'VE WON THIS ROUND, BUT I'M NOT DONE HERE."

The robot raised its hand up to head level, and only an idiot wouldn't be able to predict what it would do next.

"Uh-oh," I said.

"WHAT'S IT DOING?" Scott yelled.

"CATCH!" Professor Mayhem roared, and the robot pulled its arm back and whipped it in a blurry-fast arc, throwing Polly across the sky like a human cannonball.

CHAPTER

Stupendous took off so fast there was a real live sonic *BOOM*, then he was gone, headed up over the rooftops and after Polly. The robot turned and accelerated off in the opposite direction, and pretty soon it was out of sight too.

After a few seconds of looking at the sky, everyone started looking at each other. Max's mouth was open— I could actually see his tongue. The corners of George's mouth were pulled down so far he looked like a cartoon fish.

Everyone was talking and milling around in the street by then. Scott jumped onto another car.

"Aw, man, can somebody make him quit it?" I said.

"OFFICIAL CAPTAIN STUPENDOUS FAN CLUB!" Scott yelled.

"BWARH!" the Officials roared, more or less.

"BACK TO HEADQUARTERS! LET'S FIND A TV!"

"GRRWWWWAAAGGGHH!" the Officials yelled back, and they all took off running, weaving around cars and hooting like a giant monkey herd. Or whatever the word is for a bunch of monkeys.

"Dude, the new villain tried to kill your girlfriend," Max said. "That was mind-blowing!"

"Stupendous'll catch her," I said, totally confident. "I think—"

"Out of the way, chumps!" Scott ran right into my shoulder, knocking me into George. Max grabbed George as he tipped over sideways, which kept me on my feet too.

"Hey!" I said. Scott stopped and actually looked right past us, as if somebody right behind us had said "hey!" instead of me. Then he focused on me.

"Watch out, freak show." He smiled really wide when he said it, which made him look like a freaking kid movie star.

"Knock it off," Max said. He stepped in front of me and George.

"Or what, beef jerky? You gonna start something?"

"Come on, Scott!" some OTHER annoying kid yelled from down the street.

Scott the Annoying Kid flashed another cheesy smile

at Max, who just stared back silently. I was about an inch and a half from the back of his neck, though, and I saw it turning red.

"Later, geeks." Scott ran off toward his idiot buddies, but not too fast—he went loping off like he wasn't in any big hurry, or running away from anyone like us.

"Move it!" Ow! Another kid slammed into me as he ran by. He was wearing an Official T-shirt, of course, but he didn't stick around and talk smack like Annoying Scott.

"I swear, those guys have no respect," George said.

"You got that right." I rubbed my shoulder. "Jerks. So what about heading back into Spud's and seeing if the news has anything to report?"

"Or we could go to your house," Max said. He looked at George, who shrugged and looked at me.

"Uh, okay. I kind of wanted another slice. . . ."

"Nah, let's just go." Max smacked his hands together.

The street was full of people getting back into their cars, or trying to find their cars, but a lot of other people were just going back into whatever building they came from. We ran to my house—Spud's is on Bendis Avenue, six blocks east of my house and fourteen blocks from the bird-turd-stained apartment building where Max lives with his crazy grandmother and alcoholic father.

When we got to my house we ran behind it to the garage, aka club headquarters, went inside, and turned on the news. Patty Suarez, daredevil helicopter journalist and Stupendous tracker extraordinaire, was reporting from downtown Copperplate City, where Captain Stupendous was . . . nowhere in sight?

"The question on everybody's mind is this: Where is Captain Stupendous? Authorities say that this so-called Professor Mayhem may very well be an entirely new super-villain, but Captain Stupendous clearly had the giant robot on the defensive—it was only by hurling a bystander into the air that the robot was able to escape."

The camera cut to a clip of the robot blasting off from the battle site, taking another chunk out of the SuperSuites Hotel on its way.

Huh. Where was Stupendous?

"Where did he go?" I said in a high-pitched voice.

We all slumped down in our chairs. The camera went back to Patty Suarez.

"It's highly unusual that Captain Stupendous hasn't reappeared to make a statement about the incident. When we return: Nora Fischer is at city hall, reporting on the Copperplate Police Department's response to the incident. . . ."

George hit the mute button. We're the kind of guys

who don't talk in school, or in crowds, or at parties. Not that we ever go to parties. But around each other we never shut up. So it was a lot quieter than usual.

"This is different," George finally said. "Where did he go?"

Fan club headquarters used to be at George's house, but George's mom is . . . well, weird. She's into meditation and folk dancing, and music that's performed with trash can lids and all this other bizarre stuff, and she always tried to hang out with us. Who wants to hang out with their friend's mom all the time?

That was when I convinced my mom to let us use our garage as club headquarters. It's totally separate from the house, so it's harder for Mom to bust in on us (she still does it, though). It used to be Dad's home office, so it has its own bathroom and Internet and cable TV and everything. It also has one couch, one set of bunk beds, three overstuffed chairs, one round table, two floor-to-ceiling bookshelves, a huge collection of die-cast metal figurines, and another huge collection of action figures, including the fourteen-inch Captain Stupendous Statue with Kung-fu Grip.

"I guess they didn't find your girlfriend yet," Max said.

"They probably did, but you know they never show rescued kids on TV," I said. "And she's not my girlfriend."

"He totally disappeared," Max said.

"HE DID NOT DISAPPEAR!" I said. "He . . . he did. . . ."

"Relax, man," Max said. "There's gotta be an explanation."

That was a dumb suggestion. How could I relax after Stupendous disappeared like that?

I got up and went to the bookshelves, grabbed my gyroscope off the top shelf and brought it to the table.

"Dreidel time," Max said.

"It's not a dreidel," I said. "It's a gyroscope." I wound a string around the gyroscope's axle, pulled hard, and put it on the table to spin.

"It's more like a security blanket," George said.

"Dude, it just helps me feel calm. Don't be a hater."

"If you want a dreidel, I have a bunch at home," Max said.

"Why would I want one of your leftover dreidels?" I said.

"They're not leftovers, they're just extras. I don't need 'em, it's not like we actually celebrate holidays at my house."

"Oh, so they're sad, depressing dreidels. Even worse."

"It *could* be worse," George said. "My mom made hummus and pita bread for Thanksgiving last year. There was no turkey in sight anywhere."

"No, it couldn't be worse." Max shook his head. "Why do you think I hang out with you guys all the time?"

"Hey, there's your dad," George said, pointing at the TV.

"Yeah, that's him," I said. "Turn the sound back on." As the gyroscope slowed down it fell over with a rattle. I slapped my hand on it to stop the noise.

"Geez, I wish my dad was on TV." George had his lost-puppy-dog expression on—big, wide eyes, eyebrows turned down at the outside corners, and mouth in a straight line.

"—thank my colleagues for their unwavering support," my dad said. "Receiving the Kobayashi Genius Grant is a singular honor—"

As usual, it was both cool and bizarre to see my dad on TV. That's my dad, you know? My dad's on TV and your dad's not!

My dad is Raymond Wu—big-shot scientist, college professor, and adviser to the president. And I, the son of the big-shot scientist, am way into role-playing games, science fiction, and Captain Stupendous.

"Remember that time Mr. Grossman found out who your dad was and asked me if you were adopted?" George said.

"Which was not even a little funny," Max said.

"They should fire teachers for saying crap like that," I said. "Fire them, then maybe kick them in the shins."

My mom and dad got divorced when I was two, so I don't remember ever living in the same house with him. Every time Dad comes to pick me up for a weekend or holiday, he and Mom cross their arms a lot, snort, and say things like "accountability" and "outcomes." I'm never exactly sure what they're talking about.

"It's pretty cool that he invented superstrong fishing line," George said. "Or whatever it's actually called."

"Carbon nanotube monofilaments," I said.

"Superstrong fishing line," George said again.

"Basically, yeah," I said. "Dude, Stupendous *always*

talks to the reporters when a new villain shows up! Where did he go?"

"Why don't we ask your girlfriend?" Max said.

"SHE'S NOT—she's—wait, that might actually work."

"If Stupendous actually rescued her." George used a fake vampire voice, so he actually sounded like "Eef Stoo-PEN-dos AH-chewully RRRES-kyood her."

"He rescued her," I said.

"If he didn't, she'd be on the news," George said. "They don't care about showing *dead* kids on TV."

"I think my blood just ran cold." Max showed George his arm. "Look, I actually have goose bumps."

"Guys, SHE GOES TO OUR SCHOOL," I said. "Aren't you, I don't know . . . worried or whatever?"

That part came out a little louder than I thought it would, and the room went quiet for a few seconds while George and Max looked at me.

"Vincent, I didn't . . ." George spread his hands apart and looked at Max with his eyes wide open. "I was just kidding around, right?"

"Seriously, Vincent," Max said. "You know George. . . ." He held up his hand and flapped it open and shut like a bird beak.

"Yeah, I know, it's just, you know, a *little* bit creepy." I suddenly felt embarrassed. I coughed a couple of times, loudly, and looked down at my hands, which made my hair flop into my eyes. Max and George started pushing around their chairs and coughing too.

"Anyway, I guess we'll find out soon enough, huh?" Max held out his hand, stuck his thumb out sideways, then slowly twisted his arm until the thumb pointed down.

"Oh right, I had, like, eight seconds of happiness where I forgot," I said. "We have school tomorrow."

CHAPTER

The earth didn't fall into the sun, so, yep, we did have to go to school the next day. As usual, King Kirby Middle School was like a jungle full of man-eating tigers, only the tigers are other kids who're bigger and meaner than you are.

"Hey, Vincent, she's alive—and in school!" George said. He tried to be all secret about it by not looking, but he totally gave it away by pointing over his shoulder, right in the direction he wasn't looking.

"Stop pointing, you pinhead!" Max smacked George's hand. "She might see you!"

"Don't call me pinhead, man." George smacked Max's hand back. For just a second I felt, I don't know, like I wanted to be smacked too, but then I saw Polly and forgot about it.

Captain Stupendous has rescued a ton of people, but

this was the first time he'd rescued someone at Kirby since I'd been there, and people rescued by Captain Stupendous automatically become a little bit famous themselves. That made me want to have Polly be my girlfriend even more, actually.

"Uh-oh, Official Boy is talking to her," Max said. "You want me to take him out, Vincent?"

Max likes offering to beat people up for me, which would be nice if it wasn't so annoying. In first grade Max got his underwear caught in the zipper of his pants without knowing it and walked around like that all day. I was the only one who told him about it; everybody else just made fun of him behind his back. Max has considered himself my bodyguard ever since then, which always reminds me that as we got older, he got taller and more muscle-bound, while I actually got *more* runty.

"You never offer to beat people up for me," George said.

"That's because I think you can do it yourself," Max said.

"Oh thanks," I said.

"Vincent, look at George! He's, like, eight feet taller than you!"

"Meaning what?"

Polly came walking down the hall, with Scott the Annoying Kid next to her.

". . . so if you need any advice or anything, I've totally helped out other people who've been rescued by Stupendous. It's just part of being the president of the Official Captain . . ."

"Boy, it's just our luck that he goes to school here." I scratched my head.

"Who cares?" Max said.

"Not us," George said.

"Oh, I don't care either," I said hastily. "I'm just saying. . . ."

What a bunch of liars, right?

I tried not to look directly at Polly or Scott or anybody, but I sneaked a look out of the corner of my eye. Max was right, Polly wasn't even looking at Official Boy. She passed us (without looking over at me like I secretly hoped she would) and stopped about twenty lockers down from us.

"So yeah, I was thinking it'd be cool if you came by club headquarters and told the full membership about your experience," Scott babbled in Polly's direction. "It'd be fun, right? And—"

"No," Polly cut him off.

"Oh, come on, you know you want to."

Aaagh, I hate it when people say that.

"Sorry, I don't," Polly snapped. "I have . . . other stuff

to do." She pulled a book out of her locker, looked at it, and tossed it back in.

"Seriously, it'll be awesome!" Geez, he just wouldn't give up. "I think you totally need to come hang out with us."

"Totally not." Polly kicked her locker shut. "Look, do you mind not—"

"POLLY WINNICOTT-LEE."

Uh-oh. Mr. Castle (aka Evil Vice Principal Castle) came down the hall. He moved amazingly fast for such a squat, round person—his whole butt swiveled around when he walked. When VP Castle was a kid he probably didn't like school any more than we did, but then he went over to the dark side and became a vice principal to get revenge on the kids of the future. That's just wrong.

"Miss Winnicott-Lee, are you aware that you missed a scheduled appointment with Ms. Dryden on Friday?" Mr. Castle waved his clipboard vaguely toward the other side of the school.

"Yes," Polly said, stopping but not turning around. Oooh, the girl was seriously playing with fire. She crossed her arms and stood there with her feet apart, looking ready for a fight.

"Uh, yeah, I'll catch you later, Polly," Scott said. He tried (and failed) to look totally casual about leaving, sticking his hands in his pockets and walking away with a little bounce in his step.

"YES?" Mr. Castle raised his eyebrows, which makes it look like somebody just pinched his butt or something, but it's scary just because he can give detention. "Look at me when I'm speaking to you, Miss Winnicott-Lee."

Polly slowly turned around and looked at Mr. Castle, kind of. She was actually looking past his shoulder—I could tell, because for just a second we made eye contact, and Mr. Castle's shoulder was almost in front of her face.

I looked down.

"I'd think you could use Ms. Dryden's services even more than usual today, Miss Winnicott-Lee, considering your . . . exploits over the weekend."

"Talking to Ms. Dryden's a big waste of time," Polly said. "She's all . . ." Polly lifted one finger and twirled it around and around.

Mr. Castle brought his clipboard down fast and smacked it against the side of his leg, *WHAP!* George and I totally jumped. Max did his crazy waving-his-arms-in-the-air thing.

Polly didn't even flinch.

"Come with me, young lady. RIGHT NOW."

Polly walked past Mr. Castle with a bored look on her face, and as he turned around to follow her she rolled her eyes. She looked at me for a second and looked away, then did a double take and looked at me again with wide eyes.

"Eyes ahead," snapped Mr. Castle. He glared at us as the two of them went by. "You gentlemen need to get to class before some consequences are levied, don't you?"

Max, George, and I all looked off in different directions as he spoke, but we also pushed away from the lockers and headed off toward our next class.

"That girl's got anger management problems," George said. "You know she totally beat up Kelly Smirnoff last year, right?"

"That was just a rumor," I said.

"Totally not a rumor, I saw it," Max said. "And why was she looking at your shirt? It sure wasn't because of your muscle-bound chest." He whapped me on the chest with the back of his hand, just in case I didn't notice the original insult. I whacked his hand away and looked down at my shirt.

PRESIDENT OF THE CAPTAIN STUPENDOUS FAN CLUB.

"You're not the president, you know," George said as we went around a corner.

"What are you talking about? We voted on it, remember?"

"We just did that because you wanted to, Vincent," Max said. "It doesn't actually mean anything."

"It totally means something!"

"Vincent, I'm the treasurer." Max thumped himself on the chest with a closed fist. "But it doesn't matter, since we don't have any *money*."

"My mom told me about this thing called shared governance—the public radio station runs that way—it's where nobody gets to tell anybody else what to do and everybody has the same—OOF!"

It was actually "OOF" in stereo—I said it too when Scott and a couple of his Official Fan Club goons stampeded right through the middle of us. One of the goons bounced off Max and had to tilt his shoulder to get by, but George and I went flying like bowling pins.

"Out of the way, sidekicks," Scott said, but then he did a double take and looked at my shirt. I swear, that shirt NEVER got so much attention before.

"President of the Captain Stupendous Fan Club? That's a joke, right? I'm president of the Official Captain Stupendous Fan Club, and you guys aren't in it."

"There's no 'official' in our name," I muttered.

"What's up, Max?" Official Boy said. "Why you hanging around with these losers?"

Max just crossed his arms and stared.

"Oh, that's right, it's because you're a freak!" Scott started laughing like he'd said the funniest thing in the history of things being funny. His buddies cracked up too, and they walked away, cackling like idiot hyenas.

"I can't believe you actually used to hang out with him," I said.

"Yeah, well, that's one reason I quit the football team."

"Weirdest year ever," George said. "You were never around."

It sucked, was what I wanted to say. "Finally George and I got some peace and quiet," was what I actually said.

"It sucked," George said.

"Dude, don't get all sappy." Max reached up and rubbed George's hair, which should have looked funny since George is taller.

"Seriously, Polly can't be into a guy like that, can she?" If she was, I'd just have to kill myself.

"Forget about him, Vincent," Max said.

"Oh gee whiz, thanks for the advice, Dad."

"Dude, you have bigger things to worry about right now," George said.

Which was totally true, because we'd gotten to room 226, where we had history class, and where I was due up to give a report. Orally. In front of the whole class.

We shuffled in and took our usual seats: right side of the classroom, George and I against the wall (with George in front), and Max next to me. The rest of the zoo animals were already in their seats, which was NOT the usual thing. I scrunched my head down into my neck as we slid into our seats, but it was too late—Mrs. Burnell (our history teacher) spoke up before I could actually get into my seat.

"This is unlike you, Mr. Wu." I actually like Mrs. Burnell (she smells good, and no, I'm never gonna say that out loud to anyone) but she hates it when people are late to class. "Since you're already up, why don't we start our reports with yours?"

Somebody on the other side of the room (probably that doofus Alex Cruz) snorted, and I mentally punched myself in the face. Being late to class always makes you more visible, which makes you a target. Not even Polly Winnicott-Lee was worth that.

I picked up the five stapled pages of my report and shuffled up to the front of the room, or as I like to call it, the Terrordome, and turned to face the class.

Someone coughed a word I didn't hear, but the rest of the room obviously did. A few people laughed, and Max stared across the room at Alex Cruz, who stared back. For just a second I thought they'd get into a fight, which would distract everyone from my report, but no luck.

"Settle down, everyone," Mrs. Burnell said. "Vincent, what's the topic of your presentation?"

Is there anything as freaky as standing in front of a

classroom and talking? About anything? I took a deep breath.

"My report's about Captain Stupendous," I said.

"Again?" somebody in the class said.

Mrs. Burnell closed her eyes and rubbed her forehead. "And, Vincent, you've included—"

"A historical component, yeah," I blurted out. "I always do."

"Yes, I know." Mrs. Burnell tipped her head to the side and smiled, sort of. Her forehead was more wrinkled than foreheads usually are during a smile. "Go ahead."

Somebody made a smooching sound, immediately followed by a fart sound. There was a ripple of laughter.

I coughed, shifted from one side to the other, shifted back, and noticed how sweaty and wrinkled the report was getting where I held it.

"Like I was saying, my report's about Captain Stupendous and how Copperplate City's the only major city in the past twenty-six years with no mayor abductions." I said all that in one long breath, then had to suck in another long breath when I was done.

Just as I was about to start again the door opened and Polly came in, followed by Mr. Castle.

"Sorry to interrupt your class, Mrs. Burnell," he said. "Miss Winnicott-Lee was late for an appointment with the school counselor."

Oh dude, SO humiliating—there's nothing like having the whole class know about your appointment with the school shrink. Someone coughed the word "mental" as Polly went to her desk. Her expression didn't change, but her face turned pink. She slumped down in her chair as Mr. Castle closed the door.

"Polly's the one who should give a Captain Stupendous report." Ah, that came from evil cheerleader airhead and Stupendite Carla Bing in the back row. She was obviously jealous, if her snarky tone of voice was any sign.

"Please exercise some self-control, class." Mrs. Burnell used her emotionless robot voice, and everybody settled down. People don't mess with Mrs. Burnell when she uses that voice, no matter how good she smells.

"Sorry for the interruption, Vincent, go ahead." Mrs. Burnell nodded at me, then turned and smiled at Polly. Polly gave one of those superfast fake smiles for like a nanosecond, then slumped a little farther down in her chair.

"Out of the fifty largest cities in the country, Copperplate City is the only one that's never had a kid abducted by a supervillain," I said. "The reason is Captain Stupendous. My report is on the history of abduction attempts over the past twenty-six years and how Captain Stupendous stopped them."

I was having trouble talking because I couldn't help sneaking glances at Polly out of the corner of my eye, but when I said that last part she did something that totally threw me off. She sat up straight in her chair and looked right at me.

Like she was *listening to my report*. Which would make her the first person to ever do that . . .

CHAPTER

"I'm telling you, she was totally listening to my report! Something weird is going on with Polly."

"You sure, Vincent? Because it's probably just that post-Stupendous-rescue attack-syndrome thing, isn't it?"

I sighed. "You always get that wrong, Max."

We were at our usual lunch table, one table away from the food lines and the crabby old ladies who ran the cash register. We were at one end of the rectangle-shaped space—at the other end were all the windows, jocks, girls, Official Captain Stupendous Fan Club members, sunlight, and happiness. All the bullies and jerks were over there too, though, so there was an upside to being so close to the smelly old lunch ladies and their bad attitudes.

"Post-rescue attachment syndrome," I said. "And yeah, I guess it could be, but it was . . . I don't know, different from that."

"Because you've met so many rescued people you're an expert, huh?" George said as he stuck a Tater Tot in his mouth.

"Oh, like you have?" I shot back. George put his ketchup-smeared hands in the air.

"Look, there she is." Max nodded to his left, where the entrance to the cafeteria was. Polly walked down the ramp that went from the doors to where the food line usually started. She got to the end of the ramp, ignored the food line, and made a beeline for the girls' bathroom. She passed our table on the way and totally made eye contact with me! Of course I wussed out and looked down at the table, ignoring Max kicking my shin under the table. Polly disappeared from eyeshot, and I heard the door to the girls' bathroom close with a *THUNK* as she went in.

"Come on, man, bust a move on her," Max said.

"Shut up." I stuffed a forkful of the cafeteria's nasty Swedish meatballs into my mouth and chewed violently.

"She's totally scoping you out, Vincent." Oh great, even George was getting on my case. "Just talk to her."

"Oh right, George, like *you've* ever done that."

"What's that got to do with it?"

"This is, like, official club business, Vincent." Max clamped a hand on my shoulder. It was depressing to be reminded that Max's hand is actually bigger than my entire shoulder.

"You could—"

Every cell phone in the cafeteria went berserk with the Stupendous Alert ringtone. The cafeteria's like a giant echo chamber, so the sound of all those phones combined with everyone screaming their heads off was enough to make a guy instantly insane. I looked at my phone.

STUPENDOUS ALERT: GIANT ROBOT. KIRBY & 17TH.

"HERE! HERE! THAT'S HERE!" Geez, Scott was standing on a table *again*.

"Loudmouth," I said as we all got up from the table.

"He's right, though." George was hopping up and down. "That's practically next door!"

"It's almost ten blocks over, actually," I said. I knew that only because the school district offices, where my mom works, are right around there. I wondered if Mom could see the robot from her office window or anything like that.

"We better hurry up, then." Max cracked his knuckles.

The school loudspeakers burst into crackly, high-volume life.

"ATTENTION, KING KIRBY MIDDLE SCHOOL STUDENTS! THERE IS A STUPENDOUS ALERT, REPEAT, A STUPENDOUS ALERT! LOCKDOWN

PROCEDURES ARE IN EFFECT IMMEDIATELY!"

"LET'S GO!" Scott shouted, and with a collective "GRAAAARRRGH," every kid in the cafeteria rushed the doors. The lunch ladies didn't even try to stop anybody—one of the more leathery ones actually headed outside too.

We went through the halls of the school like a thundering herd of buffalo, ignoring the teachers who tried to slow us down.

"HALT! REPORT TO YOUR HOMEROOMS IMMEDIATELY!" I was pretty impressed by how loud Vice Principal Castle's voice was when he yelled, but he was as helpless as all the other teachers. The entire population of King Kirby Middle School spilled out the front doors of the school and took off down the street, howling with excitement the whole way.

"This way! This way!" I shouted, peeling off from the main crowd.

"This is the right way, Vincent!" Max pointed in the direction everyone else was going.

"No it isn't, there's—forget it, I'm going this way!"

Feeling pissed off, I took off running on a side street, and after a few seconds I heard Max and George following me. They caught up a half block over, and together we turned into an alley.

"Oh, really good, Vincent," Max said.

"This is a dead end too!" George shouted, skidding to a halt.

"Through the doughnut shop, you dummies!"

We reached the back door to Ye Olde Donut Shoppe, expecting its usual collection of suspicious-looking guys in ratty clothes drinking from Styrofoam cups. The shop was empty, though.

We burst out onto the next street and stopped, because the street was already crowded. All the doughnut shop guys were there, for one, and as we stopped, a bunch of other kids came skidding up behind, colliding with each other and lurching around like crazy. I got separated from my friends and ended up in the middle of the giant mosh pit that formed on the sidewalk, but I heard Max yelling "VINCENT!" from somewhere to my right.

"Ungfh!" Somebody elbowed me hard in the side.

"Out of the way, loser."

I couldn't even tell who did it—when it's that crowded the bullies all run together in an obnoxious blur.

I squirmed through the crowd, taking at least two more elbows to the ribs and a smack to the head that was probably on purpose before finding Max and George up front. Max was craning his neck to look around, and he relaxed when we made eye contact. He reached out with one big paw and hauled me in by the shoulder when I got within range.

"You okay?" he said, brushing imaginary dust off my shoulders.

I shook his hand off.

"Yeah, yeah, no worries. Where's Stupendous?"

"Dude, Stupendous isn't here."

"What do you mean?"

"I mean, he's not here, it's just the robot."

"What do you think it's looking for?"

George pointed at the robot, a block down the street at the intersection of Kirby and 17th. It was bending over and looking into the windows of the Corwin Enterprises Research and Development Lab that took up one whole block. Knowing stuff like the locations of research labs was just one of the things that made us better than the Official Captain Stupendous Fan Club, just so you know.

The robot stood up, turned around, and bent down to look in the building across the street from the Corwin Lab. That was the school district office building. Where Mom's office was.

I felt a small but weird sort of tingle in my spine, like that feeling you get when you're looking down from a really tall place—nerves, maybe? *Fear?* My mom worked in that building, after all.

What the heck was Professor Mayhem looking for?

Where was Captain Stupendous?

"You were right about the shortcut," Max said, still not looking at me.

"No kidding." I didn't look at him either. "How long's it been since Mayhem showed up?"

"At least five minutes, right?" Max said. "It took us a while to get out of the cafeteria."

I couldn't believe it. Stupendous *never* took more than a couple of minutes to show up for a villain smack down.

The robot stopped peeking into the windows of the school district offices and stood up. Its shadow was so long it covered the street behind the robot for an entire city block. The sunlight twinkled briefly off the robot's head, and I looked up and behind me to see where the sun was. That was the only reason I saw Captain Stupendous fly up from behind the doughnut shop.

"CAPTAIN STUPENDOUS!" I yelled, swiveling my head and pointing up. There was a sharp *whoosh* overhead, followed by the sound of fabric whipping in the wind. A roar went up from the crowd.

"Time to take care of business, baby!" I yelled.

A girl standing in front of me turned and gave me a why-don't-you-roll-over-and-die look, then whispered something to the girl standing next to her, who smirked.

The robot turned and raised its fists as Stupendous flew straight at its chest. He flew by too quickly for me to get a look at his face, but his fists were straight out in front of him, and his yellow cape was really bright in comparison to his blue costume. Stupendous is a big guy—six foot seven—but the robot made him look like an action figure.

"AH, THERE YOU ARE!" Professor Mayhem sounded insanely cheerful to see Stupendous.

"Game over, baby," somebody in the crowd shouted. "Watch, it's gonna be over with one punch!"

Whoever said it was wrong, though, because the robot swung one big metal fist and hit Stupendous face-first with a loud *CLANG*. Stupendous flew sideways, spun around, and crashed into the building across the street from Mom's office.

Just like that, everyone quit cheering. George, Max, and I stood there with our mouths hanging open.

"What just happened?" George said.

Captain Stupendous does NOT get hit that easily. When twenty-six Bluvian galactic battleships invaded our atmosphere and fired their antimatter missiles, he dodged every single one. When Mandible Moe attacked with his lightning-fast scissor bite, Stupendous just leaned out of the way, laughed, and knocked out three of Moe's serrated fangs. The Plutonium Brothers never touched him, no matter how many times they blew themselves up.

"ON YOUR FEET, CAPTAIN THYROID!" Mayhem hollered. "MY LITTLE SURPRISE ISN'T QUITE READY, BUT IT'S NO CONCERN. HAVE AT THEE!"

Well, that sounded very supervillainous and sinister.

"Oh, it's never good when villains talk about their 'little surprises,'" Max said.

"Maybe he's planning on blowing up the school," George said, and I couldn't help myself—a tiny streak of hope went through me when he said it.

"He's definitely got something in the works," I said.

Stupendous poked his head out of the hole he'd left in the side of the building, shook cement bits out of his hair, and launched back into the air. Then a weird thing happened—his entire body was lit up by this blue light, like there was a giant blue lightbulb inside him.

Stupendous stopped midflight and held up his glowing blue arms. That was plenty of time for Mayhem to hit him with a hard uppercut. The blue light vanished as Stupendous ricocheted straight back up in the air, flailing his limbs wildly. The robot did its Tasmanian Devil trick again—everything between its head and waist suddenly turned into a spinning blur of destruction, and Stupendous fell right into it. The robot's rotating arms hit him with a *CRACK*, and Stupendous whizzed all the way down the street. I spun around as he went by and disappeared

behind the doughnut shop. Oh, that had to hurt—it hurt *looking* at it.

The robot came stomping after Stupendous, filling the air with gigantic *CRUNCH* sounds as it ran. I spun around again to run, just as the students of King Kirby Middle School ran off in all directions, screaming and slamming into each other like deranged hockey players. My feet got tangled, and a bellowing kid in an Official Captain Stupendous Fan Club T-shirt clocked me in the head with his elbow. I went down on the pavement, with little pinpricks of light going off in front of my eyes. I thought somebody yelled "Vincent!" but it was hard to be sure—the robot was loud, and I could also hear a helicopter somewhere up in the sky.

WHAM! WHAM! WHAM! Just like that the robot was on top of me. It had a mixed-up smell, wet and metallic, and it stared straight ahead with its glassy eyes.

For a second, time slowed way down, and I was actually able to watch the bottom of one giant foot as it came down to squish me.

CHAPTER

I was in serious danger of wetting my pants when Stupendous flew in from behind, scooped me up (which kind of hurt, actually) and dragged me out from under the robot's foot. We zipped between the robot's legs, flying a couple of feet above the pavement.

The robot bent over and tried to grab us, but Stupendous did a fast midair zigzag and jetted up at a sharp angle. I saw a couple of buildings zip past my eyes, then empty sky, then a helicopter that barely got out of the way in time. Its propellers made a *WHUP-WHUP-WHUP-WHUP* sound as we flew by.

"AAUGH! Stupid helicopters!" Stupendous said. "Hang on, it's following us!"

"The helicopter or the robot?!"

The robot, of course. I looked down, and yep—it was coming after us.

"STUPENDOUS!" Mayhem yelled so loud I could hear him over the wind in my ears and the helicopter racket. "FLEE IF YOU MUST! ALL THE MORE TIME FOR ME TO CARRY ON WITH MY BUSINESS!"

What business? What was he gonna do the next day? Why wasn't Stupendous paying attention to all the warning signs?

Stupendous twitched all over, and then we were flying so fast my cheeks felt like they were stapled to the back of my head. I was positive I'd have bruises all over from being grabbed like that, plus it got colder as we got higher.

"Where are we going?" I yelled, but it came out more like "Errr aaaghwwwee oimbbb?"

The robot fell behind fast. It got smaller and smaller, but we weren't going back. Stupendous was . . . running away?

???

"Hey! HEY! THAT'S A NEW VILLAIN BACK THERE, YOU KNOW! HE'S PLANNING SOMETHING! WHAT ARE YOU DOING? HEEEEEYYYYYYY!"

Stupendous didn't hear, so I whacked him on the shoulder. That might have been a mistake—it was like whacking the side of a building. It got his attention, though, along with my scream of pain. He jerked around to look at me, and it must have thrown him off balance—before

I knew it, we were twirling around like a two-person human tornado.

When we stopped pinwheeling around I grabbed my stomach and peeked at the ground, which was really far away. The robot was nowhere in sight.

"Can we go down?" I said. I had a hoodie on over my T-shirt but it wasn't fleece or anything, and my teeth were chattering. "I don't want to catch pneumonia."

"Oh yeah. Sure," Stupendous said. He looked down for a few seconds, scanning the ground.

"That looks okay," he said, and *BAM*, we flew straight down, which meant I got to watch the ground come up at warp speed.

There's this roller coaster at Thrill Town with a harness that clamps on to your shoulders, waist, butt, and crotch, but your arms and legs and head dangle free. At one point you go over a little hill, which is where all the girls start giggling and the guys start raising their hands over their heads. Then you plunge a couple hundred feet straight down, loose body parts flapping in the wind, which is where all the girls scream like banshees and the guys do too, only they try to sound all deep-voiced and manly. I used to think that was scary.

My eyes watered like crazy. I think we hit a bird, because I heard a squawk and suddenly there were feathers plastered to my forehead. I was wondering if I'd see some kind of light before I died when Stupendous slowed down and straightened up. I felt a thump, and Stupendous dumped me on my feet. I fell over and hit my funny bone.

"Aaarrgh!" I said, which summed up my feelings pretty well. We were on a rooftop, somewhere downtown. It was warm—the best thing in the history of everything ever—and I rubbed my arms frantically.

I'm a shrimp, four foot eleven and praying for a growth spurt, but even George (who's five six) would look way up at Stupendous. If a pro football player and a Russian army tank had a baby, it would probably look like Captain Stupendous. He practically blotted out the sun. His arm was thicker than my whole body, and you could have made a decent tent out of his cape. I thought his costume would be spandex, but it was rubbery-looking.

My first time seeing Captain Stupendous up close! It should have been really, really cool, you know? Instead it was just strange, and the more he talked, the stranger it got.

"I hate those helicopters," he said. "Let them out of your sight for one second and they fly right in front of you! It's like they're trying to get killed!"

"WHAT ARE YOU DOING?" I said. I couldn't believe Captain Stupendous was complaining to me about helicopters when there was a bad guy on the loose!

"I just saved your life," he said. "You're welcome."

"You have to go back!" I said. "There's a bad guy on the loose! You know, that Professor Mayhem person?"

"What about Professor Mayhem?" Stupendous held his hands out with the palms up. "Why is he my problem?"

"YOU'RE CAPTAIN STUPENDOUS!" I yelled. "It's your *job* to catch people like him!"

"I don't know whose job it is, but it isn't mine," he said.

What was that supposed to mean? Did somebody hit him in the head with a crazy stick?

"Didn't you hear what he said? He's got some kind of evil scheme in the works, we—I mean, you have to find out what it is!"

Stupendous tilted his head and pursed his lips.

"*We* have to find out?" he said, with a tiny, little smirk.

"I said 'YOU'! When a villain says he's got something planned you have to take it seriously! Why aren't you fighting him right now? You didn't even try a Meteor Strike!"

"A what?"

"A Meteor Strike! It never fails!" I said. "It's one of your signature moves: You fly really high up, come down like a meteor, and strike with both fists! You've been doing it forever!"

Boy, you really can't tell how intense his eyes are unless you're right there looking at him. His eyes were really, really bright blue, and when he scrunched his eyebrows together his eyes looked like they were glowing.

"You think that would work?" he said.

"It's how you beat Cyclotron, remember?" I said.

Cyclotron, aka the intelligent robot from the Betelgeuse system. Powers: flight, laser cannons hidden in his arms, magnetism control.

"No, I don't remember that," he said.

"You could have done the Corkscrew Maneuver too," I said.

Stupendous grabbed at his head with both hands.

"I don't know what that is," he said.

"It's when you fly in a spiral and—"

"Okay, stop," he said, with a funny quiver in his voice.

"But why—"

"Shut up," he said.

"I'm just gonna—"

"SHUT UP!" His voice echoed around the rooftops, and I shut up. It's unusual to get yelled at THAT loudly, you know? Anyone but a psycho supervillain would have shut up.

He took a deep breath, expanding his chest to about six feet across. Then he sat down cross-legged, which I did not expect. Everything I've watched or read about Captain Stupendous shows him standing in a relaxed yet powerful pose, chin sticking out heroically, sunlight glinting in his thick black hair. Even in *Stupendous on Stupendous* (the only documentary I've ever watched all the way through without falling asleep) he always stands up. But there he was, like some kind of monk, probably sitting on pigeon crap, shoulders drooping.

He rubbed his nose with the back of his hand.

"That meteor thing, how'd you know that?"

"I watched *Stupendous on Stupendous* like everybody else. And I've read all the books. Plus I've seen every one of your fights that's been caught on video."

"What else do you know?"

"Everything. Why?"

"Why do you know so much?" he said, ignoring my question.

"I'm a founding member of the Captain Stupendous Fan Club."

I puffed up my chest, which was a little hard since I'm not exactly Mr. Universe.

"You're one of those guys funded by the Corwin Foundation?"

Big sigh.

"No, that's the Official Captain Stupendous Fan Club," I said. "We're the Captain Stupendous Fan Club, period. Not official, not unofficial, we're—"

"Okay, okay," Stupendous said. "How many members do you have?"

It always came down to membership. *Oh, there are only three of you? And you hang out all the time even if you're not having club meetings? And your headquarters is in your mom's garage and you're really just a bunch of losers? Well, you're not a real club, are you?* I guess it was predictable that the next person to shoot down our fan club would be the guy we formed the club to be fans of.

"Three."

I crossed my arms and waited for it—fake politeness, staring, or plain old laughter, I'd seen it all. But Stupendous didn't do any of that stuff. He rubbed his chin with one glove-covered hand. He stood up, and there must have been some nonfighting mojo in that superhero body, because he did it in one quick, slippery motion. It was like watching a dance move, only with more potential violence afterward. Then he said the last thing I expected him to say.

"Have you done . . . *school reports* about Captain Stupendous?"

I blinked. First of all, bizarre question. Second, Stupendous wasn't one of those heroes who liked to talk about himself in the third person.

"Yeah. About a hundred of 'em. How did you—"

He waved off my question. "What do you know about my secret identity?" he said.

Aha, he was testing me. Bring it on, Captain Rubberpants.

"I don't know anything for sure, but all human superheroes get older and fatter and uglier, except you," I said. "You look exactly the same as you did twenty-six years ago. I think this is your superhero form, but you also have a regular-person form when you're not saving the world."

DING! Oh. OH. Regular-person form.

"Something's happened to your regular body, hasn't it? It's like you forgot how to fight, or find out where you're needed, or use your powers. You don't brag and talk into the news cameras anymore."

I paused and sucked in a breath.

"What happened to you?" I said. "You're . . . different."

"Do you think?" he said with a sneer.

"What, do you have a new secret identity or something?" I was kind of joking when I said it, but I was actually on the right track!

"NO," Stupendous said, but he made it sound like "no" had three syllables, "nuh-oh-wuh," and his voice got really high. It sounded like he was lying, in other words.

"Oh wow, you DO have a new secret identity, don't you?"

"Maybe."

Dude, something really crazy must have happened.

"There's this book, *The Stupendous Paradigm*," I said. "You should, you know, read it—it talks all about the popular theories about your secret identity."

Stupendous put his hands behind his head and walked in a circle, his cape swirling.

"Can I trust you?" he said.

My palms itched, and I felt something like an electrical shock start at my stomach and run up into my hair. Captain Stupendous was about to tell me his secret identity!

"Yes."

"This might be the stupidest thing I've ever done," he said.

I literally bit my tongue.

"But I need help."

"I can help," I said. Sweat ran down my temples.

Who would the original Stupendous have picked to take over? It was probably a scientist or doctor, or someone with crime experience, like a cop. Or a college guy who didn't get a chance to do any training. Somebody old, in other words.

Stupendous muttered something and disappeared in a globe of blue fire. It was like watching a sorcerer cast a spell. Then the light disappeared, leaving a glow in front of my eyes. I pressed my knuckles against my eyelids and opened them up even though little blips of light still floated around in my vision.

?!

What?

I was wrong on all counts. Not a scientist, not a cop, not a college guy. And not old at all. Actually it was someone closer to my age. Really close. Like, also-twelve-years-old close.

And a girl.

Standing there in front of me was Polly Winnicott-Lee.

CHAPTER

Captain Stupendous was a *girl*!

There are fifty-two known superheroes in the world, including nineteen women. La Femme Invincible operates in Paris—she wears a REALLY tight costume and is extremely snotty. In Guatemala City there's La Cucaracha, one of those borderline-crazy superheroes who like to hurt bad guys more than necessary. And Gigawatt City has Hummingbird, who kicks booty with nothing but natural fighting ability, handheld weapons, and her group of anonymous sidekicks, the Hummingbird Network.

They're all grown-up women, though. None of them are girls. And none of them are as cute as Polly Winnicott-Lee.

"Hey," Polly said. "You're in my history class."

"Uhhh . . . uhhh . . ." I said, sounding like the dork of the century.

Polly looked at me with a squinty, lips-pressed-together

expression. She was about my height, maybe even a little shorter. She wore jeans with a couple of rips in the knees, a couple of earrings on both ears, and a black Radioactive Freaks concert T-shirt.

She was so cool. I've never even been to a rock concert.

"You're the one who does all those reports on Captain Stupendous, you're . . . Francis?"

Ouch.

I cleared my throat. "I'm Vincent." I managed to say it without squeaking. "So, am I right? Are you not the original Captain Stupendous?"

"Yeah—no—I mean, yeah, you're right, and no, I'm not."

"So how did . . . what did you . . ."

"It's complicated."

She rubbed her eyes, and I noticed they were a little red. If Captain Stupendous got smacked in the face by a robot, did Polly get bruised? Her face didn't look bruised. I didn't know how it looked. Frustrated, maybe. Or lonely.

"How do you know about our club?" I said.

"Well, there's that T-shirt." She pointed at my chest. "And all those reports were a pretty good clue."

"And you know about the Official Captain Stupendous Fan Club too."

Polly snorted.

"It's hard not to know about them, especially now that Scott Fanelli won't quit stalking me."

I felt a little stab of jealousy, like I'd just been poked in the side with a fork. *Scott Fanelli, you are now my sworn nemesis.*

"We're way better than them," I said. "We can totally help you—"

"How are you any different?"

"We study Captain Stupendous," I said. "They don't know anything about you! A lot of kids only join that club because they do stuff like go to baseball games. We sat behind a bunch of the Officials at the Bouncing Boy Diner once, and one guy didn't even know who Killjoy is!"

"Yeah, well, I don't know either."

I slapped myself on the forehead.

Killjoy, aka Giuliano DeShields. Powers: flight, super-strength, laser vision, emotion manipulation. His specialty was busting up happy occasions like weddings and birthday parties.

"He's one of the worst bad guys anywhere," I said. "They've been duking it out for years."

I stuck my hands up in the air, the same way the bad guys always do when they get caught.

"We've read every Stupendous book ever written, we've

looked at every picture and every video, and I've written eleven reports on him for school! You think those airhead Stupendites have done that?"

"We go to school with a couple of the Stupendites," Polly said. "You know Carla Bing? And Lucy Sakai? They *are* airheads."

"Exactly," I said. Carla Bing and Lucy Sakai were actually *evil cheerleader* airheads. In sixth grade they started a rumor that I had lice—for no reason—and *everybody* believed it. It was like they'd passed out a candy-flavored brainlessness potion that the whole class chugged at once.

Polly had a gap between her front teeth, which I found myself staring at. It wasn't huge, like somebody who had a tooth knocked out; it was just a skinny little gap that a toothpick probably wouldn't fit through.

It was kind of cute, actually.

"Are you looking at the gap in my teeth?" she said, with her arms crossed.

Rats.

"Uh, no, I, um . . . hey, do you want to meet the other guys in the club?" I said.

"No."

I blinked a couple of times. "Why not?"

"Look, I'm not interested in joining your little fan-boy

club, okay? I just need some help figuring out what to do about . . . you know, this superhero thing."

Max and George would *kill* me if I didn't get them in on the action. Well, not George, but definitely Max. Besides, this was HUGE. No way would I try to fly solo on something this big.

"We can totally help you, but we can help you more if it's all of us," I said.

"Well, I—"

"I know, the reports and all that, but the guys, they're like, my *partners*, you know? We work together."

"I only—"

"Plus this has never happened before, right? You want all the help you can get, right?"

I was talking faster and faster, and Polly raised both her hands in the air.

"Okay, fine—"

"Seriously, with all of us—"

"OKAY, OKAY! I SAID, OKAY!"

I stopped and took a few deep breaths while Polly looked at me, hands up, leaning slightly backward.

"Fine," she said. "I'll talk to you AND your friends. Just stop flipping out."

"Cool," I said, trying not to flip out any more than I already had. "Club headquarters is at my house, it's—"

"Not at your house," Polly said.

"It's actually my gara—"

"Whatever, I don't want to do it there."

"Why not?"

"NO, okay? Not until I get a chance to know you and your friends a little more. This stuff is all too . . . I don't know, private and weird. I don't want to go to anyone's house."

"Okay, where, then?"

"I know a place."

CHAPTER

Polly—Captain Stupendous—Polly Stupendous?—after Polly turned back into Captain Stupendous and took me back to school I did some thinking. The man/girl thing was way too confusing. When Polly was in Polly form, I'd call her Polly. When she was in Captain Stupendous form, I'd call her Captain Stupendous, or Stupendous, or the Big Chin, or something. The only other option was to let my brain explode.

Captain Stupendous (not Polly) said he had to go home (Polly's home! Oh my head), so we both stared at the ground for a little bit, then he flew off. School was mostly deserted, but Alex Cruz and a couple of his caveman buddies were hanging around in the parking lot.

"What up, loser?" Alex yelled as I walked by. I know, so original!

I was relieved to see that the doughnut shop was still

in one piece, even if it was kind of scuzzy, but there was plenty of damage to the buildings down the block, so they'd obviously closed the place up. I got out my phone and called George, and when he picked up he sounded so excited that my phone almost blasted a hole right through my skull.

"VINCEEEEEEENT!" he yelled. "We're at Spud's, get over here!"

I rode as fast as I could to Spud's, which was totally crowded again, of course. George practically mugged me when I walked in the door, and Max gave me a double high five when I got to the table. George was literally jumping up and down with impatience. A pizza with a few slices gone sat there on the table.

"You're alive, man, that's awesome!" Max said.

"Yeah, it's better than being dead."

"I don't think so, HAR HAR HAR. . . ." a random bully said as he walked by. At least he didn't stampede right through me, like the bullies whose names I actually know.

"Dude! Dude! Dude!" George said, over and over. George looks incredibly goofy when he's excited, his face is all buggy eyes, buckteeth, and eagle-beak nose.

"Will you calm down?" I said. "Have they sent out a truancy report yet?"

People ditching school is a very common thing during Stupendous battles—everyone gets the Stupendous Alert on their phones, and kids just bolt, trying to get to the battle scene and watch. Mom's talked to me about it a thousand times—about a thousand times more than I wanted her to—and the school district has never found a way to stop it, because teachers aren't allowed to actually tackle kids or anything like that. And it's never been a problem, because Stupendous always keeps kids who watch the battles out of trouble. Not *one* kid's ever been killed or badly hurt during a Stupendous battle! It's kind of mind-blowing when you think about it.

Of course that was when I realized how close I came to being the first, and I suddenly felt a little dizzy.

"I don't think they're even gonna do a truancy report." George was grinning like a fool. "They didn't take attendance before closing the school, they just told everyone to go home as fast as possible!"

"I doubt anyone noticed you were grabbed by Stupendous," Max said. "It was crazy how fast it all went down, you know? We didn't even know you were gone until they told everybody to go home—we waited for a while, but you didn't show. So we came here to wait it out."

Max took a slurp of soda.

"WHAT HAPPENED?" George said. "AFTER HE RESCUED Y—"

"Keep it down!" I said in a loud whisper.

"Why?" George said. "You should tell everyone!"

"You might even impress that girl you like, Polly What's-Her-Name," Max said.

I snorted.

"Probably not," I said.

"Dude, don't be such a, what do you call it, pissimist," Max said.

"Pessimist," I said.

"Whatever," Max said. "She'd totally be impressed! The only reason to keep it secret would be—"

Max's eyes opened up all the way, all at once, and George knocked a plastic cup over. It ricocheted off a chair and went rattling away across the floor.

"You know something," George said, his eyes open extra wide.

"What did he tell you?" Max said.

"All kinds of amazing stuff," I said. You know that feeling when you know a really good secret, and other people don't know it but they know you know it? It was awesome.

"Tell us!" George said.

"Dude, chill," Max said. "He'll tell us when he's ready."

I waited for it, and sure enough, exactly two seconds later Max said, "Okay, Vincent, you're ready NOW."

I told them almost everything—the crowd knocking me over, getting picked up by Stupendous, flying to a downtown rooftop, telling Stupendous about the Meteor Strike, etc. George let out many cries of "dude!" and "excellent!" and "what?" as he pounded me on the back, while Max sucked on a toothpick and occasionally raised both arms in a touchdown signal. When I got to the part about Stupendous telling me his secret identity, I thought George's head might explode.

"This. Is. AMAZING," George said. He was whispering, but it was almost as loud as his regular voice, just more hissy sounding. "It's the biggest secret ever!"

"I know, right?" I said.

"So who is he?" Max said. "What's his secret identity?"

"You're not gonna believe it," I said. I leaned way over the table and whispered, "It's Polly Winnicott-Lee."

"WHAT?" he said.

George spoke in a lower voice. "She's a *girl*!"

"A girl he's in love with," Max said. "Don't forget."

"I'm NOT in love with her." I punched Max on the arm. He didn't react at all, as usual.

"Dude, this is getting crazier and crazier," George said. "A girl? How can Captain Stupendous be a girl?"

"We have to meet up with her, Vincent," Max said.

"We are," I said. "This afternoon, at Lake Higgleman."

"Lake Higgleman?" George and Max said at the same time.

"Wow, could she pick a more disgusting place?" Max wrinkled his nose.

"That's probably the only lake in the world that people avoid on purpose during the summer," George said. "Wait a minute. . . ."

"I think I can hear the gears grinding in your head, George," I said. "Yeah, it's private."

My phone rang (the non–Stupendous Alert ring) and I checked to see who it was before answering.

"Hang on, guys, it's my dad. I'm surprised it took him this long to call.

"Hi, Dad."

"Hi, son, where are you?"

That's my dad. He's lived in Copperplate City his whole life and nothing bad's ever happened to him, but every time a villain comes to town he has to call and make sure the villain didn't show up specifically to kill ME.

"I'm at Spud's, Dad."

"Maybe you should head home, son. I was in the lab so I didn't see the news right away, but that robot attacked the school district offices!"

"I know, Dad."

"That's practically next door to your school!"

"I KNOW, Dad. I actually go to that school, remember?"

"You didn't go out there to watch or anything like that, did you?"

Sigh. "Everybody did, Dad."

"Patty Suarez reported that a student was almost killed during the fight!"

The key word is "almost," I wanted to say. "I've got Max

here to protect me." As usual, Dad totally missed the sarcasm.

"Max can't protect you, Vincent. Everyone in this town overestimates the level of protection provided by Captain Stupendous, especially when it concerns unpredictable new villains like this Professor Mayhem character."

I don't know where he was getting all that stuff about the city not being safe, but whatever. Except . . . maybe now he was right? Ugh.

"I think I'll come by for dinner tomorrow night. Sound good to you?"

"Sure. Can we, um, not talk about . . ."

"About what?"

"You know . . . chemistry and science and stuff like that."

As soon as I said it I wanted to take it back, but it was already out there. Sometimes I wonder if I really am as dumb as Dad thinks I am.

"Vincent, you can't talk about Captain Stupendous twenty-four hours a day. A little academic rigor is good for you."

"Dad, I—"

"You're not too young to think about the future, you know."

"I was just—"

"Be the hero of your own life, Vincent!"

Sigh. "Ooooookay, Dad. Forget I said anything."

"I'll call your mother right after I get off the phone with you. I'll see you tomorrow, son."

"Okay, Dad, see you."

"STAY OUT OF DANGER."

"Sure thing, Dad." I stuffed my phone in my pocket. I should say I *started* to stuff the phone in my pocket, but it rang again. Mom, this time.

"Hi, honey, are you okay?"

"I'm totally fine, Mom, are *you* okay? That robot was right outside your building!"

"I'm okay, I was actually downtown for a meeting when the robot . . . well, I wouldn't say it attacked the district offices, exactly. But most of the district leadership was in the field anyway, so if this Professor Mayhem was looking for one of us, he would have been out of luck in any event."

"Okay. Are you . . . coming home?"

I looked at Max and George, who were staring up at the ceiling, with their hands folded in front of them and mouthing *no, no, no, no, no, no, no.* Seriously, we had work to do, and Mom coming home and being a helicopter parent wouldn't help. Lucky for us, Mom has never been a helicopter parent.

"I'm afraid I have to stay here, Vincent. The mayor has called an emergency meeting—"

"—of the city leadership in response to the latest Captain Stupendous incident," I said along with her. Yeah, Mom is actually enough of a big shot to get called into those meetings, and there are a *lot* of them. She chuckled a little bit.

"Are you sure you're okay? Your father would probably pitch a fit if he knew I wasn't coming home to spend the afternoon with you, but . . ."

"It's cool, Mom, don't worry!" I tried not to sound too happy. Nothing makes a parent more suspicious than being happy when they say they won't be home soon.

"Okay. I should still be home in time for dinner, though, and remember that Bobby's coming over tonight."

"Okay." I hung up and shoved the phone back in my pocket. "Detective Bobby Carpenter's coming over for dinner tonight."

"Awesome!" George was very impressed by cops. "That's so cool that your mom's going out with a cop. You think he'd let us look at his gun if we asked?"

"No, George." I was 100 percent sure the answer was no—I'd already asked to see Bobby's gun, and he said no. But he didn't start treating me like I was a dumb, irresponsible kid, which was a nice change of pace.

"Let's just get out of here," Max said. "It doesn't sound like anything else'll happen today."

"Whatever Mayhem's planning will happen soon, though," George said. "What do you think he's gonna do?"

"I guess we're gonna find out," I said. "Let's go to the lake, we've got a date with Captain Stupendous."

CHAPTER

We left the mob of Stupendous fans inside Spud's, hopped on our bikes, and headed out. We rode through Auto Row, past Chinatown, through the Copperplate University campus, and finally into Higgleman Park. The park is full of baby strollers, grandmas with two canes, freaks with sandwich boards talking about the end of the world, and girls on Rollerblades.

The south end of the park is ringed by hills and covered with big rocks and scrubby trees. The hills look out over Lake Higgleman, one of the grossest places in existence. It is covered by an inch-thick layer of algae, and a million geese live there, honking and breeding and crapping like there's no tomorrow. If Lake Higgleman were in a more central spot, the smell would probably kill everyone in the city.

"She couldn't find a nice Porta-Potty to meet up in,

huh?" Max said, wrinkling his nose and pulling his shirt down in back. Wearing tight shirts like Max does means your shirt always rides up in back when you're on a bike. One more reason to wear baggy shirts, I say.

"I guess not. Let's go up there," I said, pointing at a nearby hilltop covered with twisted-up trees. We walked our bikes up the hill, weaving and picking up one wheel or the other to avoid all the goose turds.

"If we weren't about to meet Captain Stupendous, I'd smack you upside the head, Vincent," Max said, hopping a little as he stepped on a turd. "This is too much like being at home."

"Hey, this was her idea," I said. "Blame Polly."

"You could . . . I don't know, clean up your house more, you know," George said.

"I keep telling you, it's more complicated than that."

George shrugged. "I do it."

"I *can't*—dude, you've met my dad. Why are we still talking about this?"

George shrugged again. "Sorry."

We got up into the trees and, holy mackerel, there was a clear space with almost no bird feces in it, just a bunch of big, flat rocks. We tilted our bikes up against the gnarly devil trees and stood in a circle, looking at each other. Then we sat on the rocks and waited. We thought

about going down to check out the water, but seriously, the goose poop made the whole place like a toxic-waste dump.

"Okay, where is she?" said Max after two minutes.

"Here," Captain Stupendous said. He stepped out from behind a tree, straight in front of me and right behind Max. He must have been waiting there the whole time. His hair was all black and shiny, and the *S* below the *C* on his chest gleamed.

Stupendous tapped Max on the shoulder, and Max twitched once really hard and flailed his arms in the air. He does that waving-his-arms thing every time he's surprised—if we're at the movies and a monster jumps out of the shadows, he does it. Sometimes it's hilarious but mostly it's just strange. Stupendous took a step back.

"Whoa, what is that all about?" he said.

I kind of wanted Stupendous to make a more dramatic entrance—flying in at warp speed, coming up out of the ground like a human drill, etc.—but the guys were definitely impressed. They looked like somebody just hit them on the back of the skull with a board. Stupendous muttered "stupendify," and there was a BLIP of blue light. Polly appeared.

"Wow," Max said. "You really are a girl."

Something was wrong with Max's voice—it was, I don't

know, less monotone than usual? His hair is impossible to smooth down—too spiky—but he ran a hand over it anyway. His hair sprang back up immediately.

"Congratulations, genius," Polly said. "Figured that out all by yourself, huh?"

"This can't be for real," George said, wrapping his arms around his head.

Polly looked at George. "What do you mean?"

"It's just, you know . . . how can a girl be Captain

Stupendous?" George said. "Captain Stupendous is supposed to be a man."

"SUPPOSED to be a man?" Polly said, giving George a full-on look of death. George took a step back.

"Well, I just mean he's always *been* a man."

"I think it's cool," I said. "It's unexpected, you know? Nobody's gonna guess Captain Stupendous is a girl. And we have more important things to—"

"Why won't anybody guess Captain Stupendous is a girl?" Polly said. She looked at me and put her hands on her hips. "Why can't a girl be a superhero?"

"Hey, don't get mad at me," I said. Geez, you try to say something helpful. . . . "It's not my fault you're a girl."

"Girls are, you know, girls," George said. "They like dolls and makeup and ponies and stuff like that, not superheroes."

"Oh little dude, wrong thing to say." Max shook his head. "What George means is—"

"They? You know you're talking to an actual girl, don't you?" Polly said. "You can tell the difference, right?"

"I think it's okay that you're a girl," I said.

"Oh, well, thank you so much," Polly said. "I don't know why I bothered meeting you guys, I knew it was a dumb idea."

"Fine, go lose another fight by yourself, then!" I said.

"Maybe I will!" Polly said.

I smacked myself in the forehead, then took a deep breath.

Polly looked at Max and George. "Who are you guys anyway?"

"Oh right," I said. I introduced George and Max.

"Hi," George said.

"Hey, Captain Stupendous's new alter ago," Max said.

"You *look* normal, but you're pretty weird, you know that?" Polly said to Max, ignoring George.

"Why do you think I hang out with these guys?" Max said. He grinned, and for the first time I noticed how straight and white his teeth really are. I poked the back of my snaggly canine tooth with my tongue.

"I thought it's because we were the only ones who'd sit with you during lunch after that underwear-in-the-zipper thing in first grade," I said.

"DUDE." Max frowned at me, neck muscles bulging. "SO uncool."

"I'm just saying."

"That was only because you guys were so weird nobody else would sit with you either," Max said. He grinned again, but it was wider and more sharklike—you could see more of his teeth.

"So did you become Captain Stupendous after the first fight with Professor Mayhem?" George said, darting his eyes back and forth between me and Max.

Polly nodded, but she kept smirking at Max. "You remember how the robot just threw me, right?"

"Totally," I said.

"It's a classic distraction move," Max said.

"Throw a helpless victim, then make a clean escape!" George said.

"Will you guys shut up?" Polly said. "It's like you're talking about sports."

"Um . . . we don't like sports. . . ." George said.

Polly ignored him again and glared at us for a minute.

"I totally screamed and thought I was gonna die, but Captain Stupendous caught me and took me to this random rooftop.

"He asked me if I was hurt, and I said no. I was kind of surprised—on TV he seems so stuck-up, but he was really nice. Then he looked like he was gonna fly off, but he just stood there with one hand in the air. After a second he disappeared in a flash of blue light. Another person appeared in his place, grabbed his chest, and fell down. I couldn't tell who it was at first, but then he said my name. Guess who it was."

George, Max, and I looked at each other.

"How are we supposed to know?" Max said.

"You probably knew him too!" Polly crossed her arms.

"Did you take that art enrichment class in fourth grade?"

"MR. ZAZUETA?" I said. "No way!"

"Way," Polly said. "Mr. Zazueta was Captain Stupendous.

"He waved for me to listen to him—I had to put my ear right over his mouth. He said he was having a heart attack, and he didn't want to do it this way, but there was no choice. Then he grabbed my leg and said something I couldn't hear, that harsh blue light was everywhere, and he said, 'Now you're Captain Stupendous.'

"Then he died."

The clearing was quiet for a minute as we thought about that. George even managed not to make some kind of creepy joke about dead people.

"I took a bunch of Mr. Zazueta's classes." Polly's voice was low, and she was looking at her feet. George opened his mouth to say something—probably something dumb—but Max punched him in the shoulder. "He was the only teacher in our school who wasn't a total idiot."

"I guess he was cool," I said. "I didn't really know him."

"Was he your *friend* or something?" Max said.

Polly shrugged. "I talked to him about stuff—art, or my mom and dad. Sometimes I . . ."

"Sometimes you what?" I said.

"Nothing," Polly mumbled, closing her eyes and taking a deep breath.

Captain Stupendous was an art teacher. Dude, what a letdown. And Polly talked to a teacher about her *family*? It was like she lived in an alternate universe.

I guess all three of us were just staring at Polly, because she looked quickly at each of us. Max smiled, George kept staring, and of course I looked down at my feet. When I looked back up, Polly was standing with her hands in her back pockets.

"So those other clubs suck and you guys are the real experts, huh?" Polly said.

We nodded. We weren't being stuck-up, it was just the truth.

"We know the things that really count," I said. "Fight moves, refinery accidents mapped against mutant events, villain attack patterns . . ."

"We know everything," George said. Max crossed his arms and nodded his head. "Well, except Max." Max glared at George and held up a fist.

"Do you know how to get 'rid of the powers'?" Polly said.

Confusion! Did she really say that? George blinked really hard, and Max twitched just a little bit.

"What do you mean, 'get rid of the powers'?" I said.

"I mean, give them to someone else, like Mr. Zazueta gave them to me," Polly said. "I don't want to be Captain Stupendous."

CHAPTER

Don't want to be Captain Stupendous? What kind of crazy talk was that?

"You don't want to be the most amazing superhero that's ever lived?" George said.

"Why should I?" Polly said.

"It's obvious," Max said. "So you can beat anyone in a fight or save the world! So you can fly!"

"I already know how to fight, and I don't care about any of the other stuff," Polly said.

"Why not?" I said.

"Oh, I don't know, because it SUCKS?" Polly said. "Because I don't LIKE fighting giant robots? Because my life is already full of crap I'm SUPPOSED to do, instead of stuff I actually WANT to do?"

"I don't get it," George said. "Who wouldn't want to be Captain Stupendous?"

"Her, obviously." Max pointed at Polly with his thumb.

"He didn't ASK me!" Polly said, her eyes closed into angry slits. "He always . . . he . . ." She took a deep breath and her eyes suddenly drooped down at the corners. "He always asked me about stuff, instead of just telling me to do it. But this time he didn't ask, he just did it."

"But . . . but what about keeping the city safe?" I said. "You heard Professor Mayhem, he's planning to spring some kind of surprise attack! If you quit, who's gonna stop him?"

What would I do if Captain Stupendous wasn't around anymore? Seriously. Being a Captain Stupendous fan was pretty much my whole reason for being alive.

Polly's forehead crinkled up, and she clenched her jaw.

"Somebody else," she said.

I wondered if the transfer of powers caused brain damage or something.

Max held his arms open and gave a really broad smile, like he was a game show host greeting the crowd.

"No worries, I'll do it," he said. "Give the powers to me."

George started jumping about three feet straight up. He pumped his hand over his head at the top of each jump, and his mouth was open in a perfectly round O shape.

"No, no, me, me!" he said. "Give 'em to me!"

"Wait a minute," I said. "It can't be one of you guys,

SHE was handpicked by Captain Stupendous to be his successor!"

"Well, dude, we know it's not gonna be you," Max said. "Have you ever seen yourself try to punch somebody? It's embarrassing to watch."

"Shut up, Max," I said. I punched him on the shoulder, but he just flicked at me with the fingers of his other hand, like he was brushing away a mosquito.

"See?" Max said.

"You do hit like a girl, Vincent," George said.

"WHY ARE YOU GUYS BEING SO MEAN?" I yelled—I mean, it was like *BAM*, somebody'd just poured a bucket of angry juice over my head.

Max and George both leaned away from me, George with his mouth open and Max with his mouth puckered up and his eyebrows bunched together.

"What's going on?" George said to Max.

"I dunno. What's with you lately, Vincent?"

"What's with me lately is how you guys have been ganging up on me! What's your problem?"

"Dude, calm yourself," Max said. "We don't have a problem."

"I should just beat up all three of you," Polly said, and that broke the tension because she sounded pissed off enough to actually try. "Do you know how to do it?"

"How to do what?" All three of us said it at the same time.

Polly grabbed her hair with both hands.

"GET RID OF THE POWERS," she said.

"No," I said.

"We didn't even know it was possible," George said.

"Mr. Zazueta did it right in front of you, didn't he?" Max said.

"I DIDN'T HEAR HOW HE DID IT," Polly said. "The only thing he actually told me how to do was to say 'stupendify' to change back and forth. Were you dummies listening to anything I said?"

"I guess you're stuck," I said.

"What a rip-off," George said. "It should totally be one of us, guys are just stronger than girls—no offense."

"What?" Polly said, with a squinty-eyed look.

"I said, you'll get more respect as a man than—OW!"

Polly punched George twice in the arm at lightning speed, *POW, POW.* They weren't just regular punches either, there was something *Enter the Dragon* and chopsocky about the way she balanced herself and made fists with both hands. George rubbed his arm and looked at Polly like a kicked puppy, with his eyes all big and droopy at the corners.

"You hit pretty hard for a girl," Max said, with new

respect in his voice. George turned the kicked-puppy look on Max.

"I can hit harder than that," Polly said, cracking her knuckles. "I've been taking karate for six years. I can kick three boards in half."

"THREE?" Max said. "Wow! Vincent can't even open a jar of pickles by himself!"

I tried to kick Max in the shin, but I, um, missed.

"Thanks," I said, hoping Polly couldn't see how red my face actually was. "Thanks a lot, Max."

"Vincent, you gotta lighten up, I'm just messing with you."

"Right. Just messing with me."

"Could you hit a guy in the solar plexus if you had to?" George said, looking a little less mopey. "I hear you can kill somebody that way."

"Yeah, I know where the solar plexus is," Polly said.

"Huh," George said. "Maybe you actually could take on Professor Mayhem."

Polly sat down on a rock and put her hands on top of her head.

"Why would I want to do a stupid thing like that?" she said.

"You have to," I said. "You HAVE to, Polly."

"I don't HAVE to do anything." Polly put her hands on her knees and gave me a dirty look. "I have enough people thinking I'm a freak without turning into a DUDE IN SPANDEX."

"We'll teach you how to be Captain Stupendous. You have to do it," I said in desperation.

"Seriously, Polly, supervillains are really big on warning superheroes about their evil plans," Max said. "It's like they all have a disease that makes them brag about all the details of their plans ahead of time."

"My mom would probably say it's a personality disorder," George said.

"If Mayhem says he's got a surprise for you, he'll

definitely spring it soon," I said. "You gotta be there to stop him."

"What about other superheroes?" Polly said. "Atomic Aardvark or somebody like that."

Atomic Aardvark, secret identity unknown. Powers: flight, radiation control, radiation resistance. According to witnesses he's kind of a jerk.

"I don't know about you, but I'm not friends with Atomic Aardvark," Max said.

Polly and I stared at each other, eyeball to eyeball.

"This is like fate or something, isn't it?" George said, looking at Max and cracking his knuckles. His voice went way up on "isn't it?"

"It's like destiny," Max said, with his arms crossed and his head slowly nodding. He was also giving Polly another really wide smile. Max does *not* smile that much in regular life. I shook my head, and—AHA!—thought of the PERFECT thing to convince Polly.

"What do you think Mr. Zazueta would say?"

Polly crinkled up her forehead and looked away. "I don't care what he'd say, but he'd probably say something like you have to do what's right for everyone, but only if it's right for you."

"Every man for himself, huh?" George said. "Mr. Zazueta should hang out with my dad."

"Dude, no," I said. "That's not it at all."

"No, it's not." Polly actually agreed with me! Ha! "He wasn't like that. I told you, Mr. Zazueta was cool."

She took a couple of steps back and looked at me again. "What would *you* do?" she said.

"I know what I'd do, I'd—" Max started, but Polly cut him off.

"I'm asking Vincent."

Well, now, that was interesting. Of course I'd dreamed about being Captain Stupendous like every other kid in Copperplate City, maybe in the whole world.

"I don't know," I said. "I guess I'd do it."

"You *guess*?" George said.

"Why do you say 'I guess'?" Polly said in a hard voice. She put her hands on her hips.

I was figuring out what to say as I said it, so I talked real slow.

"Because . . . it'd be a big deal, right? Not just because of the responsibility and stuff, but because it's, like, you *knew* him! As a regular person, not a super-hero. It's . . . I don't know, it's different because of that."

"I don't get it," George said.

"But I'd still do it. Because the world still needs Captain Stupendous."

There were two beats of silence, then Max reached over and clapped me on the shoulder.

"Yeah," he said.

"Okay," Polly said. "Tell you what, I'll give you a chance to change my mind—ONE chance—but only on one condition."

I didn't let out a sigh of relief or anything—the situation was still twenty-two varieties of messed up—but I felt better knowing Polly wouldn't just cut out the center of my entire existence. Or, you know, let Professor Mayhem destroy the city or whatever.

"Name it."

"Don't try and recruit me to join your little club." Polly crossed her arms. "I don't *join* stuff. Got it?"

Well, what a pisser. Why wouldn't she want to join us? Still, it was better than having her brush us off completely.

"Okay."

"So what do we do now?" George said.

"I better go home," Polly said. "My mom's showing a house at three, and she'll freak out if I'm not there when she gets home. She's been really twitchy since the robot-almost-killing-me thing."

"Can't you tell her you're hanging out with us?" I said. "Tell her about the club."

Polly hooted. "Oh yeah, that's not gonna freak her out."

"Let's meet up at club headquarters tomorrow, then," Max said.

"Yeah, let's . . . I was about to say that." I didn't exactly give Max a mean look, but it wasn't a friendly look either.

Polly changed into Stupendous form and flew off.

"What's your deal, Vincent?" Max said as soon as Stupendous was gone. "You're being superpissy, it's bumming me out."

"Me too," George said, standing slightly behind Max.

"*I'm* bumming *you* out?" I couldn't believe my nubby little ears. "You guys have been all 'oh, we went to the beach without you,' and 'oh, Vincent's being so touchy,' and 'oh, let's just do this and totally ignore Vincent again.' Why are you being so bossy about everything?"

"I'm not being bossy." Max crossed his arms and knitted his eyebrows, which of course made him look totally bossy.

"You are being a *little* touchy," George said to me.

"I AM NOT BEING TOUCHY."

We made the long ride back to my house in silence. When we pulled into my driveway there was a cop car parked there, which instantly made things less tense—after superheroes, nothing gets the conversation going again like cop cars.

"Is that your mom's boyfriend's car?" Max said.

"Yeah," I said. "She said he was coming over for dinner."

"Do you think he'd let us do a ride-along sometime?" George actually pressed his forehead against the window of the cop car as we looked in.

"I don't know," I said. "Probably not."

"Your mom would lose it if you rode along in a cop car," Max said.

"Well, you know, peace, love, and understanding and all that crap. Unless she's breaking up with a boyfriend or girlfriend—then it's like global nuclear war," George said. Max patted him on the back, but in a gentle way, not in his usual violent way.

There weren't any handcuffs or shotguns or anything good in Bobby's car, so we stopped looking. George and I leaned our bikes against the house while Max just let his fall over with a crash. We went straight to club headquarters for a debriefing session.

"What are we gonna do tomorrow?" George said, flopping into a chair.

"We should totally show Polly some battle clips," Max said. "To, you know, make her understand how awesome Captain Stupendous is."

"What about Cloudsplitter?" I said.

"Nah, we gotta start with Cyclotron," Max said. He sat

down and put his feet up on the table. "Giant robot then, giant robot now. Totally makes sense."

I resisted the urge to slap my forehead at the continued bossiness.

"Yeah, but the battle with Cloudsplitter was more cool," George said. Thank you, George! "We have to show her how cool it is to be Stupendous, don't we?"

"We don't have enough time for that," Max said.

There was a knock on the door, and like usual, Mom opened it without waiting for an answer.

"Hi, boys," she said.

"Hi, Ms. Keller," George said.

"Hi, Vincent's mom," Max said in his new manly-man voice, sounding . . . okay, he actually did sound older. Dumbest way ever to say hi to somebody's mom, but Max thinks it's funny.

"Mom! How about waiting for us to let you in?" I said. She completely ignored me, of course—no reason why she should be different from anyone else; she's only my MOTHER.

"Bobby'll be back with dinner any minute, Vincent, it's time to get ready."

"Okay, Mom. How about waiting for us to let you in? Hello?"

Mom ignored me and shut the door, and Max and

George dragged themselves out of their chairs reeeeeally slowly.

"What are you having for dinner?" George said, with hope in his voice.

"Sorry, guys. Mom specifically told me this is family only."

"Bobby's not family," George said.

"Yeah, well, when you start dating my mom you can call yourself family."

"I would totally date your mom," Max said, with a grin.

"AAAAAUUUGH!" George and I said in unison.

"Dude, that's my *mom* you're talking about! Cut it out!"

"And stay away from *my* mom," George said, with a shudder.

"Is your mom even home tonight?" Max asked George.

George shrugged. "It's not like I don't have a key. You sure we can't stay, Vincent? Maybe I could get Bobby to take us for a ride!"

"Sorry, dude. Mom's really big on having Bobby and me, you know, bond." I actually was sorry, but not too much since, except for Mom, I'd have Bobby to myself. "Tomorrow, guys," I said. "We have to get Polly on board with being Stupendous, and fast."

CHAPTER

For a long time my least favorite four-word phrase was "dinner with Mom's boyfriend," but Bobby broke that streak. I usually find out pretty quickly how lame Mom's boyfriends are, because I'm forced to hang out with them. Bobby isn't creepy, he doesn't try to be like a dad, and he gets to carry a gun. He is actually kind of cool, unlike Mom's ex-boyfriend the dentist, who tried to get me to like him by giving me free toothbrushes.

I ran out into the yard, up the back steps, and into the house. Mom was closing her laptop on the kitchen table when I came in. She brushed a little bit of hair off her forehead. In my baby pictures her hair is all the way down to her shoulders—it looks really blond in those pictures—but she was just a teacher back then. She got one of those old-people-style haircuts when she got her first job as a school principal. Someone once told me my mom looks

young for her age, but it was one of my teachers, who was probably even older than my mom. Old people like to talk about how young other old people look. Mom gave me a hug, and I let her do it.

"Where's Bobby?" I said. "His car's in the driveway."

"He wanted to get some exercise, so he walked over to Excelsior Pizza. He'll be back any minute."

Score! Detective Bobby Carpenter was getting a head start on racking up brownie points. "Hey, Mom, did you know Mr. Zazueta at my school?" Who DIED right before school started under mysterious circumstances? *I* thought they were mysterious, anyway.

"I did, actually," Mom said. She rubbed her eyes with the back of her hand. "Miguel was a good man."

"Were you, like, friends or something?"

"We weren't terribly close, but, yes, I considered him a friend." Mom sighed. "We went to high school together, you know."

I didn't know that! "So Dad knew him too?"

"Yes. It's probably been hard for you at school with him being gone."

Uh, no, not really . . .

"I guess."

"I'm so sorry," Mom said. "Anyway, this Professor Mayhem is bound to fail, Vincent. Captain Stupendous will handle it."

I wasn't so sure, and I could tell by the crease in her forehead that Mom wasn't either, but I didn't get into it.

"Sure," I said. "Is Bobby working on the Professor Mayhem case?"

"Bobby's part of the team handling it, yes," Mom said. "He has experience collaborating with superheroes. Did I tell you he was involved in the capture of Jane Don't?"

Jane Don't, aka Geraldine Holtz. Powers: sonic shriek, superspeed, the ability to spit daggers. Seriously, when she spits, it automatically turns into a tiny, sharp dagger. She was only caught because Hummingbird is really good with daggers.

"I already knew," I said. "That's so awesome that he worked with Hummingbird."

"I'm glad you think so," Mom said. "Bobby was the police department's liaison with Hummingbird—I think he has similar hopes for working with Captain Stupendous."

REALLY, NOW. Veddy interrrresting.

"Bobby likes you, you know."

"That's cool," I said as the doorbell rang.

"Speak of the devil," Mom said.

I headed for the dining room while Mom went to the front door. I heard the sound of her and Bobby's voices getting closer as they walked through the living room, then Mom came into the dining room with Bobby right behind her. He had a big, flat box from Excelsior Pizza (not as good as Spud's, but not bad) in his hand, and it smelled tasty—the box, not his hand.

"Hi, Vincent," Bobby said. He stuck out his hand. "How are you?"

"Hey, Bobby," I said. Mom gave me a stiff-fingered ninja poke in the back, and I stuck out my hand too. Bobby grabbed it, squeezed once, and let go. Mom poked me again.

"Uh . . . how are you?"

"I'm fine, thanks for asking," Bobby said. "You like sausage and mushroom, right?"

I blinked. "Right!"

I thought detectives wore regular clothes—they always do on TV—but Bobby always wore a standard cop uniform. The dark blue uniform, combined with his dark skin, created some high contrast with our blinding white living room. It was like an optical illusion.

"I hear you're a big fan of Captain Stupendous," Bobby said as we sat down at the table. He loaded up a plate with three slices and handed it to me. Dad always gives me one slice at a time.

"The biggest," I said. I bit the point off my first slice, stretching the cheese out a foot from my face. "Idd oo reary . . ." I sucked in some air to cool down the pizza. "Did you really meet Hummingbird when you were working in Gigawatt City?"

"I really did," Bobby said. He bit the point off his own slice, while Mom blew on her slice to cool it down first. She was smiling, looking back and forth between me and Bobby.

"What's she like?" I was really curious—it tripped me out that somebody like her, with no superpowers, could still be a superhero.

"She's, well, she's very businesslike." Bobby laughed. "I guess you have to be, in that line of work. But she has the highest integrity, and treats people with a lot of respect, which is something *I* respect. Don't be too impressed, though—mostly I communicated with the Hummingbird Network."

REALLY! Now that was the kind of stuff I liked hearing about!

"No kidding?" I said.

"No kidding," Bobby said, with a smile. "I've always thought municipal police departments should have stronger collaborative relationships with civilian groups like the Hummingbird Network—you'd be surprised by how much valuable information they can dig up."

"That's so cool."

"Thanks," Bobby said. "I think it's cool that you're such a big fan of Captain Stupendous."

"Huh," I said. "Really?" Some adults don't think it's cool at all—Mr. Castle, for example. Or my dad. Or any teacher I've ever had. Or any adult I've ever met in my life except for Bobby.

"Captain Stupendous has provided the highest level of law enforcement the world has ever seen," Bobby said. "He does the right thing. Why shouldn't you admire a man like that?"

"You're not worried about him?" I said. "I mean, after he ran away from that fight and everything . . ."

"I'm concerned, yes," Bobby said. "And I'd like to know more about the situation. But I have faith in Captain Stupendous. He'll be back."

Bobby was awesome! We spent the rest of dinner talking about the Stupendous situation, Professor Mayhem, and other stuff Bobby'd done in Gigawatt City, like setting up a local office for the Federal Department of Villain Containment Services. When it was time for Bobby to leave I was actually sorry to see him go, and you know something is different when I can say that about anyone I know through my mom.

"I'm always happy to talk more about Hummingbird and Captain Stupendous, Vincent. I won't always be available to talk right away, but you can call me, okay?" Bobby said as we walked back into the living room. He pulled a card out of his pocket and handed it to me.

"Bobby, that's very sweet, but do you really think it's a good idea?" Mom said.

"It's fine, Violet," Bobby said. "Someone did the same for me when I was a kid, I never forgot it."

"Uh, okay," I said. "Thanks." I looked at the card, then stuffed it in my pocket.

Bobby smiled at my mom, and I looked over my

shoulder at her too. She was smiling at Bobby in that way where she crinkles up one corner of her mouth, which usually means she thinks something's funny, but in a good way. I guess it was because Officer Bobby and I were bonding.

"I should go," Bobby said. "Good to see you, Vincent."

"Good to see you," I said, and it was weird to actually mean it. Cool, but weird.

"Thanks, Vincent," Mom said. This time she smiled just at me.

"Sure," I said, not feeling any big urge to watch them hug or, *blech*, maybe even kiss. Mom and Bobby headed for the front of the house, talking about "citywide protective measures," which was cool because citywide protective measures always mean no school.

"Is school closed again tomorrow?" I said, half shouting as I walked back through the kitchen.

"Yes," Mom shouted from two rooms away. "And please stop shouting!"

I went back out to headquarters and wondered if I should clean up or something—an unprecedented thing was about to happen, after all. A *girl* was coming over.

CHAPTER

"Check it out, Mom's boyfriend gave me his business card," I said the next day when George and Max arrived. "Pretty cool, huh?"

"My mom's boyfriends do that sometimes, but they're all, like, organic farmers or union leaders and stuff like that," George said. "Like I'm ever gonna call anyone that boring."

"I'd totally call Bobby! We talked about Hummingbird and Captain Stupendous all night, it was awesome."

"Sweet," Max said. "You're lucky, Vincent. You have a dad who's not a loser AND a mom with a cool boyfriend. It must be fun."

"Well," George said, "it also sounds like not as much fun as hanging out with Captain Stupendous, even if he is a girl."

"Speaking of girls, girls are not into die-cast metal

figurines, guys," Max said. "Or role-playing games or science fiction. We gotta hide all this stuff."

George and I grabbed him as he started digging around on one of the shelves, sweeping stuff into his arms.

"Cut it out, Max," I said.

"Our stuff is awesome!" George said. "I don't even know what you're worried about!"

"Vincent, your girlfriend is coming over," Max said.

"She's not my girlfriend!"

"You sooooo want her to be your girlfriend," Max said.

"It's true, Vincent," George said, nodding his head.

"Will you guys get your heads in the game?" The lack of focus is incredible, right? "Professor Mayhem? Polly? Right?"

"That's why you have to make the most of this chance," Max said. "For all you know, this might be the last time a girl ever comes over here."

"Since when are you such a big expert about girls?" I said.

"Since I made out with Jessica Shoop last year, that's since when."

"Noooooo," George said. "ONE kiss from Jessica Shoop doesn't make anybody an expert."

"She probably kissed you on the cheek or something,

right?" I was totally jealous of Max, but no way was I gonna admit it.

"I'm so jealous." I swear, George has no pride.

"Total make-out session." Max was very calm, which was annoying because it made it sound like he wasn't lying.

"Look at you, you haven't even taken a shower," I said. "You look like a squirrel made a nest on your head. Why would anybody make out with you?"

"Because I'm irresistible, dude," Max said.

"Could have fooled me," Polly said.

Everyone jumped—it was like a spastic synchronized swimming move. Polly stood in the doorway, which we had left open to let in some fresh air.

She wore a baseball cap, big mirrored sunglasses, a bandanna around her neck, and another concert T-shirt—Kamikaze Fighter Pilot, whoever they were. Her hair was in a ponytail.

"What's Kamikaze Fighter Pilot?" George said.

"A band."

"Cool name," Max said, polishing his fingernails on his shirt.

Polly looked around the room—the bunk beds, the computers, the dusty barbells in the corner, the forty thousand science fiction novels on the shelves, the superhero posters on every wall, and the shelves full of Captain Stupendous action figures.

Our headquarters is so cool! Max was nuts.

"Have a seat," I said.

"Okay," Polly said. She came and sat down at the table, which would have been fine if she hadn't taken the chair I was about to sit in. George and Max slid into the other two chairs really fast, so I had to stand there like an idiot. I went into the closet, dug out an old folding chair, and squeezed it in between Polly and Max.

"Dude, what are you doing?" Max said.

"How about you guys give me a little more room?" Polly said, holding her elbows tight against her sides.

"Sorry." After a bunch of scooting around and kicking each other's chairs, we settled down. The folding chair creaked as I sat in it.

"So I've been thinking," Polly said. "I was talking to my friend Lily last night—"

"You didn't tell her about you being Captain Stupendous, did you?" I said, suddenly worried.

"Yeah, you have to protect people from knowing too much," Max said.

"NO, I didn't tell her. How brain-damaged do you think I am? I was just asking her what she *thinks* about Captain Stupendous."

"Is she one of the Stupendites?" George perked up.

"George has a thing for the Stupendites." Max pointed at George with his thumb.

"Oh dude, you totally have a thing for Lucy Sakai!" George swatted Max's thumb away.

"It's totally cool that you like the Stupendites, George," Max said.

"Lily's not a Stupendite, she's just someone I know from—she's just someone I know."

"Someone you know from where?" George said.

Polly sighed.

"From the Captain Stupendous Rescued Teen Support Group, okay?"

"The what?" Max said. "Do you know about this group, Vincent?"

"Yeah, it's like a . . . well, a support group. For people who've been rescued by Stupendous and . . . um . . ."

How do you say "people who've been rescued by Stupendous and are freaking out over nearly dying" without getting punched in the face? Because, seriously, Polly looked ready to punch me in the face.

". . . and just need to talk about it with other people with the same deal." I felt like an idiot saying that, but Polly seemed to relax, so I guess it worked.

"Yeah, what's her name, Ms. Dryden, at school put me in touch with them. Most of the people in the group are lame, but Lily's cool, so I asked her what she'd think if there was no more Captain Stupendous."

She said everything would suck, right? I thought.

"She said that would really suck, because she was . . . I don't know, grateful or whatever that he saved her life."

"Well, duh," George said. "I mean, YOU'RE grateful, right?"

"Yeah, I just . . . I don't know." Polly frowned, which didn't make her look even a little bit grateful.

"You don't know what?" Max said.

"I don't know what to do!" Polly threw her arms into the air. She managed to NOT smack me upside the head, but it was close.

"It's obvious, isn't it?" George said. "Be Captain Stupendous."

"Stop Professor Mayhem's plan, whatever it is," Max said.

Don't take away the best thing about my life, I almost said.

"I don't owe you guys anything, you know!" Polly was practically yelling, which made me a little twitchy since I didn't have any experience with angry girls who know karate.

"I didn't say you owe us anything," George said. "Nobody owes anybody anything."

"The cops would probably be psyched to get a little help, though," Max said. "People in this town aren't used to dealing with stuff with no Captain Stupendous."

"IF I DO THIS, IT'S ONLY BECAUSE I WANT TO!"

Polly actually yelled that time. George leaned away from her, and Max's eyes were open so wide that his eyebrows were almost on top of his head.

"Okay, you're, like, a really freaky chick," George said, still leaning as far away from Polly as he could.

Holy cow, Captain Stupendous's alter ego was terminally pissed off. It was tough to see that as a good thing.

"Why are you so mad?" Max said.

"I'M NOT MAD." Polly crossed her arms in a really hard, violent-looking way.

"Oooookay . . ."

"I don't get something," I said.

"Which thing are we talking about this time?" George said.

"Oh, HAR DE HAR HAR—excuse me, but I'm talking to *Polly*. If you're so mad about being Captain Stupendous, why'd you go fight Professor Mayhem the other day?"

Polly shrugged and ran both hands through her hair.

"Because . . . it's gonna sound stupid. . . ."

"Because of Mr. Zazueta," I said in a quiet voice.

"Because he got it, right?" Max said.

"Because he was your friend," George said.

Polly looked at us one at a time—Max, George, and finally me. Then she blinked a few times, really fast, and rubbed her eyes hard with the back of her hand.

"Yeah," she said. "I didn't want to be a total loser and not even try."

"So . . ." I said after a minute. "Do you want to?"

Polly took a deep breath and blew it out.

"I don't know."

"Is that a yes?" Max said.

"I guess."

Aaaaaaaaahhhhhh. Sweet relief—Captain Stupendous would fly another day. I was so relieved I put my hand up for a high five. Polly stared at it for a second and smirked a little, but she eventually smacked her palm against mine.

"Where do we start?"

CHAPTER

"We start with video," I said, opening up my laptop.

We reviewed Captain Stupendous's greatest hits, including Cyclotron AND Cloudsplitter. A sound engineer recorded Cloudsplitter fighting Stupendous in the Financial District, and Cloudsplitter kept saying stuff like, "You are no match for me! After I've destroyed you I'll kill the mayor and eat his children!" Then he'd hurl a lightning bolt at the Captain's head. Hilarious!

"Why do I have to turn into a man?" Polly said after an hour of Meteor Strikes, Double Helixes, Corkscrews, and Mole Attacks.

"Who knows?" Max said.

"Because Captain Stupendous is a man," George said really slowly, like he was talking to a baby. "Duh. Ow!" Max punched him in the arm.

"Watch the snark level, man. There's a girl in the house." Max smiled at Polly, and she rolled her eyes.

"There are a lot of theories," I said, secretly happy about the eye rolling.

During the early Stupendous years there wasn't much video, but there've always been pictures. Over time there were more pictures, and eventually tons of video, and in all of that stuff he looks the same—build, costume, hair color, and gender. Huge, blue and yellow, black, and male.

"Some people think Stupendous is an alien with no secret identity at all," I said.

"There's another theory that says he's a vampire!" George said.

"Not a regular vampire, but one who isn't hurt by the sun, can't be staked in the heart, doesn't drink blood, and isn't bothered by holy water," I said.

"In other words, not a vampire," Max said. "Worst theory ever."

"Now that we know you're Captain Stupendous, only one theory makes sense—you must be switching bodies," I said. "Probably the Stupendous body is kept in some interdimensional holding tank."

"Like those ministorage places you see from the freeway," George said. "Except in another dimension."

"When you make the change your regular body goes there and your mind goes into the Stupendous body," I said.

"Okay, but why can't I stay a girl?" Polly said.

"Who knows?" George said.

"That's crap." Polly flopped back into her chair. "I like being a girl."

I secretly liked her better as a girl too.

"It's not enough that my dad wishes I was a boy, now the entire universe is actually *making* me be one."

"My mom likes to say, 'gender is a construct of society' and stuff like that," George said. "Sometimes I think she wants me to be a boy *and* a girl."

"Is your dad Asian?" I asked Polly. "Because that would explain it."

"Yeah, but he's not, like, eating kimchi all day and stuff, he's totally American—he just really wants a son. My mom's not Asian, but I have the opposite problem with her." Polly's eyes were half-closed, and she let her head roll back on her neck until she was staring at the ceiling. "She wants a super *girly* girl. With lacy dresses and glittery makeup and all that garbage."

"Parents suck," Max said.

"And their weirdo friends too," George said, with a nod.

"Yeah. So . . . you guys know there's no way I can fully

learn all these moves in less than, like, six months, right?"
Polly said.

"You have to," I said.

"Why don't you kung-fu fight the robot?" George said.
He did a funky, circling motion with his hands and kicked
one foot out to the side.

"I tried to do some before the last fight," Polly said.
"But the ground is a big deal when you do karate. When
I fly I can't push off with my feet, plus everything with
that stupid body is messed up—the arms and legs are too
long."

"You should at least learn the most important moves,"
I said.

"Definitely the Meteor Strike," Max said.

"The Corkscrew too," I said.

"The Whirligig is really cool," George said, pinwheeling
his arms around his head.

"OH, OH, you gotta learn the Tumbleweed," Max said.
"The Tumbleweed is aweso—"

"AAAAGH!" Polly's scream made us all jump, except
for Max, who did his crazy flailing thing and whacked me
in the ear.

"Stop it!" Polly said, holding her head.

"Okay, maybe not the Tumbleweed," Max said. "Geez,
calm down."

"Maybe we should get out and do some practicing for real," I said. "You need flying practice, and we can't do that in here."

"Good idea," Polly said. "I've watched all the video I can stand. Some sparring would be good."

"We can do that anywhere," Max said. "As long as it's private."

"Let's go back to the lake," Polly said.

The room erupted in boos and hisses.

"What? It's private, isn't it?" Polly said.

"Yeah, but it smells like a dead dog's butt," Max said.

"We can go there if there's no other place, but do you really want to deal with the stink if we don't have to?" I said.

"Okay, you guys are the experts, you think of a place around here!" Polly said.

"Why do we have to stay around here?" I said.

"Where are you thinking, Vincent?" Max said. "Watertown? Africa? Mars?"

"Why not?" I said. "We have Captain Stupendous right here! Is there a reason why we can't practice anywhere we want?"

"I guess not," Max said.

"Yeah, just call me Captain Taxicab," Polly said.

"You don't actually want to go to Mars, do you,

Vincent?" George said. "It'd be cool, but we'd need space-suits. . . ."

"George . . . NO, I don't actually want to go to Mars," I said.

"I'm not taking anyone to Mars," Polly said. "I don't care if you guys want to go or not."

"Okay, then, where?" Max said.

"It's so obvious," I said. "We should go to Colossal Dome."

CHAPTER

Getting to Colossal Dome turned out to be uncomfortable, of course.

"I can't believe we're going to Colossal Dome," George said as we jostled for position inside my mom's old toolshed. "Do you think any of the Nexus of Infamy's weapons are still there?"

"No," Max said, digging his elbow into my side.

"Stupendous cleaned all that stuff out after the final battle," I said.

"Vincent, you're invading my space," Max said.

"I'm invading your space? You're kidding, right?"

"You know what, it's probably just me getting bossy. That's me, Boss Max."

"Boss Max is a good villain name," George said.

"Shut up, it is not," I said.

We don't spend a lot of time stuffing ourselves into

dusty, old toolsheds, but we needed a way for Captain Stupendous to take us to Colossal Dome without being seen. We were a mile over Copperplate City, packed into an ancient plastic toolshed that Stupendous carried. It was one of those tall, skinny ones, about the size of a closet, so it was pretty cramped in there. Our backpacks and messenger bags were piled on top of our feet, so we were constantly losing our balance and falling into each other.

Yeah, I know. A plastic tool closet being carried by a flying superhero? Not very secret. But at least nobody could see it was me, Max, and George inside.

"Is this stealing?" Max said.

"It's not stealing if the thing is owned by my mom," I said. "Can you not stand on my foot like that?"

Colossal Dome is at the top of Mount Chancho, the highest peak in the Copperplate Mountains. Mountain climbers used to love the place—it was one of those legendary, superhard mountains that only a few people could climb all the way to the top. Then the Nexus of Infamy decided to build its headquarters there.

I knew we'd arrived when the whole toolshed went WHUMF and tilted. We bounced, smacking our arms on the plastic walls. The door was yanked open, and George toppled to the ground at Stupendous's feet. Max and I picked up the backpacks and tossed them over George's body. Just for fun we stepped over him as he tried to crawl out of the way.

"Stupendify!" Polly appeared in a flash of blue light.

"If I was Captain Stupendous, I'd never change back," George said.

"Yeah, well, I like being myself," Polly said.

"This place is HUGE." Max craned his neck and looked up at the ceiling.

Colossal Dome is—well, colossal. The dome's a quarter mile across at its base, and five hundred feet high at the top. The Nexus of Infamy website is actually still live, so even though I'd never been there I'd already seen pictures. On the website, the dome is filled with death machines, tanks of man-eating alien dolphins, and interdimensional portals and stuff, but in real life it wasn't like that at all. There was a bunch of rusty metal piled up right next to the north end of the dome, but other than that it was mostly dirt, weeds, and a few scrubby trees.

We'd landed right in the middle of the dome floor, which had some grass mixed in with the weeds. There was plenty of sunlight. It actually wasn't that different from being inside a baseball stadium, except for being bigger.

George and Max were running toward the wall—they were probably racing—so Polly and I looked around.

"You guys were right, there's plenty of room," Polly said. "Are you sure nobody comes here?"

"Positive," I said. "You saw the sides of the mountain, right?"

"Yeah, it's like somebody just chopped off the sides and turned the mountain into a rectangle," Polly said. "What about other bad guys?"

"Nope," I said. "The whole world knows about it now that the Nexus is out of business. Bad guys like secret hideouts. Hey, that looks like a decent spot to set up."

I pointed at George and Max, who apparently weren't just racing each other like idiots. They stood on a big cement platform halfway between the center of the dome and the pile of rusty metal. They waved their arms over their heads, and George jumped up and down a few times.

The platform was two or three city blocks away, so it took a couple of minutes to march over there. Polly and I threw all the bags at George's and Max's feet. George jumped straight up and Max hopped sideways to avoid them.

"Thanks for helping with the bags, guys," I said. "Jerks."

"I'm just trying not to be bossy, dude," Max said.

"This must have been the Nexus launchpad," George said, totally ignoring me. "Cyclotron actually took off right from this spot!"

This was our first time doing a remote superhero fighting technique practice session in a former supervillain hideout, so we brought a ton of stuff, including my laptop and video camera.

We dove right into teaching Polly how to fight like Captain Stupendous. We watched a lot of clips and talked about a lot of battles, which was fun because we ALWAYS watch clips and talk about battles. After each clip Polly changed into Stupendous and tried out the fighting move from the clip, while we filmed her with my video camera and picked apart her technique.

"You can't keep changing back into your regular form," George said as we watched a clip of the Yo-yo Maneuver. Polly didn't even bother looking at him when he said it.

She was really good at copying the moves. I kept looking at her out of the corner of my eye—not to be all secretive; I just didn't want to embarrass her. While we watched Stupendous doing the Mole Attack against Galactica Minor, I looked at her sideways, and realized she was looking at me sideways. I instantly looked at the ground, but I'm pretty sure she smiled when we made eye contact. It was fast—BLINK, smile, and BLINK, gone.

After a couple of hours we took a lunch break. When the sandwiches and doughnuts were gone, Max and George actually did race each other from one side of the dome to the other. Polly and I sat cross-legged on the edge of the launchpad.

"Did you see the police helicopter on the way here?" I said.

"No, for once," Polly said. "Why?"

"It's just a surprise that they're out there," I said. "There was this bad guy called Blitzkrieg who blew up three police choppers ten years ago, and ever since then they've been really cautious about going up during Stupendous battles."

"Somebody must have changed their mind about it," Polly said.

Bobby, I thought. "There are a bunch of new cops in town," I said. "From Gigawatt City. They helped catch Jane Don't."

We watched Max and George, who'd already raced from one side of the dome to the other and were running back the other way. George was in the lead and pulling away—Max is stronger, but George is superskinny and lightweight. He's like a human greyhound.

"This is messed up," Polly said. "Me being a superhero, you guys showing me how to be a superhero—it's a joke."

"Kind of," I said. "What else can we do, though? And don't tell Max, but you're definitely a better superhero than any of us would be."

I was looking right at her when I said it, so I know for a fact that Polly smiled for another nanosecond. Then BLINK, gone. She was, like, the fastest smile in the west, but it was kind of nice to know she wasn't pissed off ALL the time, even if the smiling part made me nervous in a totally different way.

"So . . . um . . ." You know how you try to think of something to talk about and your mind turns into Jell-O?

"I guess you guys have been friends forever, huh?" Polly watched as George reached the wall, way off in the distance, then passed Max coming back the other way.

"I've known Max since preschool," I said. "We didn't

become really tight until first grade, though—that's when George and his mom moved here. They lived in Watertown until his parents got divorced."

"We moved here when I was in third grade," Polly said. "My mom got a job with Morrison Realty. That's why my dad's gone so much—HIS job is still in Watertown."

"Really? Watertown's pretty far from here."

Polly smiled, a no-teeth, no-happiness kind of smile. She tapped my temple with her finger, and I managed to stop myself from flinching more than a tiny bit.

"Brains. He lives there during the week, so he's only home on Saturdays and Sundays. And he plays golf all day on Saturday."

The sound of thudding feet got gradually louder as George and Max ran up. George jumped, landed on the launchpad with one outstretched foot, and shot past Polly. She twisted away from him and leaned into me, almost knocking me over.

Max hit the launchpad two steps after George and pulled up, bending over with his hands on his knees.

"YEAH!" George stuck his arms straight up in the air and did a spastic little dance. "I win! GEORGE WINS!"

"Hey, I'm generous." Max stood up, still breathing hard. "I'll let you have this one victory, little dude."

"Oh, don't even get into the little-dude stuff, I totally beat you!"

"Hey, guys, I think we should call it a day," I said.

"Why?" Max said. "There's a lot more stuff to look at."

"Dude, the clock's ticking. What if—"

I was interrupted by a creaking, grinding noise over by the wall that Max and George had just raced to and from. It sounded like somebody dragging a big rock across a cement floor, if the rock was the size of a car. It was too far away to see for sure, but it looked like the ground was moving.

"Aw, that can't be good," I said.

CHAPTER

Polly and I stood up. Polly clenched her fists.

"You guys, did you see anything over there?" I said. "Like maybe an old supervillain booby trap?"

"Nope," George said. "Just this big crack in the ground."

"It was actually a really big crack," Max said.

"What happened to this place being totally cleaned out?" Polly said.

"Um . . . we were wrong?" George said.

"What kind of stuff did the Nexus of Infamy have stored underground in here?" Max asked.

"Nothing I know about," I said.

"WHAT DID YOU GUYS DO OVER THERE?" Polly yelled.

"We didn't do anything!" George said. "We just jumped over this crack in the ground, that's it!"

The grinding noise stopped, but was replaced by a series

of deep, clanging sounds, with a metallic screech every so often.

"It must be some secret alarm system that Stupendous missed," Max said. "Probably nothing to worry about."

"Nothing to worry about, ha," I said. "Do you even know where we are? THIS IS COLOSSAL DOME! The headquarters for the Nexus of Infamy! Who knows what's down there?"

"WELL, IT WAS A PRETTY STUPID IDEA TO COME HERE IN THE FIRST PLACE, WASN'T IT?" Max said.

"I DIDN'T HEAR YOU COME UP WITH ANY BETTER IDEAS!" I said.

"OH, DO YOU ACTUALLY WANT ME TO? OR WOULD THAT BE TOO BOSSY?"

That's when the giant laser cannon came up out of the ground.

BAMF! I didn't even hear Polly speak, but I saw the flash of blue light and suddenly Captain Stupendous was there. Polly's arm hadn't been anywhere near me, but when she changed into Stupendous, his elbow almost took off my head.

"What is it?" Stupendous said. It was weird to hear that deep man voice right after hearing Polly's high girl voice.

"Do you recognize that thing, Vincent?" Max said in

a quiet voice. There were two wavy furrows across his forehead.

"Nope," I said. "What do you guys think?"

"Death ray of some kind, right?" George said.

"Well, yeah," I said. "What kind of death ray is the question."

"When did Stupendous get so sloppy?" Max said. "How do you completely miss an automated death ray buried in the ground?"

"Death rays, you mean," Stupendous said. He turned in a slow circle, pointing, and we all heard the grinding sounds as three other death rays came up out of the ground. The death rays were right at the base of the walls, evenly spaced around the dome's perimeter.

"This must be the backup defense system or something," I said.

"They look rusty," George said.

They also looked huge. The death rays were so big we could see them pivot in our direction, and they were so rusty we could hear them squealing as they pivoted. They looked a little bit like the cannons in old war movies, except they were a hundred times bigger and had glowing red cables wrapped all around them.

"Yeah, it's more like the backup system for the backup system," Max said.

The air was split by a *SIZZLE* and a *ZOINK*, and the four death rays each fired a laser beam. Max, George, and I screamed and hit the deck—I left a nice little patch of elbow skin on the cement when I landed—and the lasers hit Stupendous dead center.

They didn't do a thing, of course. Captain Stupendous is totally immune to lasers, which came in handy that time Laser Man attacked the city. Stupendous just stood there with four big spots of red on his upper body and one thin beam reflecting off his chest logo.

"Huh," he said. "This doesn't even hurt." He bent down and let one of the lasers hit him right in the eye. "I don't feel a thing. This is kind of cool."

"Great!" I said, squinting at the guys with one eye. Max had his hands clasped across his head, and George was curled up in a ball. "It's gonna hurt if we get hit, though, so can you deal with those things?"

"Oh right, sorry," Stupendous said. "I guess this is a perfect chance to try out some flight maneuvers."

"WHATEVER!" Max yelled. "JUST TURN OFF THE DEATH BEAMS BEFORE THEY HIT US INSTEAD OF YOU!"

WHOOSH! I felt a breeze as Stupendous launched. I twisted my head sideways and cracked open one eye just in time to see him do a perfect corkscrew around one of the laser beams and hit the big laser cannon, smashing it into pieces.

"YEAH!" he shouted, and it was so loud I thought I saw the remaining laser beams vibrate in the air. "METEOR STRIKE!"

Stupendous went straight up, flying through the dome so fast it looked like a Stupendous-size hole just appeared there by magic. At almost the exact same moment a second hole appeared on the opposite side of the dome, and another one of the laser beams over our heads blinked out.

"WHOOOOOOO!"

There's nothing like the sound of a superhero screaming

"whooooo" at the top of his lungs—I thought my ears were gonna explode as Stupendous zipped over and took out another laser cannon with a *CRUNCH*. The last cannon tried to track him, but the laser beam couldn't keep up. It wasn't even close.

Stupendous zigzagged across the dome like a human lightning bolt and destroyed the last cannon with a *SKRUNCH*. We looked up as he thumped to a landing on the platform.

"That was awesome!" he said. "Did you see it?"

Stupendous's grin was HUGE. It was different from how he used to grin, though, pre-Polly. It was just as toothy, but there was more of an angry-eyebrow thing going on.

He looked a little scary, to be honest.

"Uh, no," George said. "I was distracted by being afraid of dying and all that."

"Do you guys play music?" Stupendous said.

"Yeah, I play bass drum and Vincent plays clarinet," George said.

"I don't think marching band is what he's talking about, George."

"There's this amazing rush you get when everybody hits the same groove at the same time, it was kinda like that." Stupendous played a couple of seconds of air guitar, and somehow made it look cool—I look like a giant dork when I play air guitar.

"Those stupid lasers didn't hurt at all." Stupendous spread his arms open, as if the lasers were still hitting him.

"Duh," Max said. "You're immune to lasers, everybody knows that."

"Which is really weird, when you think about it," I said. "Lasers should hurt a lot more than robot punches."

"Yeah, what's up with that?" Stupendous said.

"Lasers are made of light," George said. "Robot punches are made of, you know, robot fists."

"Yeah, but taking out those death rays didn't hurt at all," Stupendous said. He waved his hands in the direction of the demolished laser guns. "They're made of metal too, right?"

"Old, rusty metal," George said.

"They weren't 100 percent rust," Stupendous said. "They were still mostly metal, and punching them felt totally different from punching the robot. The robot felt way harder."

"'Harder' like 'not easier'?" George said.

"No, 'harder' as in 'not softer.' Punching the robot hurt more than punching the laser guns."

"Maybe Professor Mayhem invented some kind of inde-structible metal," Max said.

Yeah, right, I almost said, but I realized the idea wasn't all that crazy.

"The robot is pretty freaking cool," I said. "Anybody who could come up with something like that probably *could* invent an indestructible metal."

"Your dad invented an indestructible something," George said. "Unbreakable silly string, right? If he could do it, Mayhem could do it."

"That would be bizarre, wouldn't it?" Max said. "If Professor Mayhem and your dad both invented some kind of indestructible gizmo at the same time?"

"I guess," I said. "My dad's invention is a string, though. That's pretty different from a robot."

"Whatever, guys," Stupendous said. He sat down, crossing his legs and leaning backward on his arms. "So if you think Mayhem's robot is indestructible, does that mean if we fight again, I'm just totally dead?"

Yes, I thought.

"I don't know," Max said.

"Probably," George said.

"No," I said. "Dude, what's your problem? Of course not. And it's just a theory anyway."

"Who knows when that nut job is gonna do something crazy again?" Stupendous said. "It could be any minute. He could be out there doing something crazy right now!"

"Yeah, but look at it this way," I said. "If Mayhem's robot really is made of some indestructible metal he invented himself, that must mean you're not as bad at fighting as we thought!"

"That's true," Max said. "You didn't know how to fight like Captain Stupendous, right?"

"I'm really good at fighting," Stupendous said. "I'm just bad at being a freaking superhero."

"But now you have some of the moves down," George said. He stood up and did another one of his half-funny, half-lame fake karate moves. "You actually can fight like Captain Stupendous now."

"Sort of anyway," Max said.

"So that means you've evened up the odds," I said. "If you can fight more like Captain Stupendous—"

"Combined with your karate skills!" George said. He did some kind of spazzy fake bird kick, flapping his arms like wings and kicking straight out in front of him.

"—then the only thing we have to worry about is how to destroy a robot that might or might not be indestructible!" I said.

I realized how stupid that sounded right after saying it, just so you know.

"Yeah, sounds like a piece of cake," Stupendous said. "Stupendify."

BAMF! And there was Polly, legs crossed, leaning backward. She leaned forward, put her elbows on her knees, planted her forehead on her hands, and stared straight down.

"I'm dead," she said. Then she slammed her fists down on her legs and said, "AAAUGH," totally startling the rest of us. She jumped to her feet and started pacing.

"What I need to do is find a way to kick his butt when he's NOT hiding inside his toy robot like a big loser!"

"Good luck with that," George said.

On that sarcastic note we decided to play it safe and hustle out of Colossal Dome, because who knew what other crazy leftover evilness was still there? Plus, all of our parents wanted us to come home for dinner that night.

We piled all our stuff into the toolshed and climbed in, grumbling and stepping on each other's feet. When we took off, Max elbowed me in the side and George stepped on my ankle, but I forgot about that when all three of our phones rang at the same time. That could only mean one thing, and looking at my phone confirmed it:

STUPENDOUS ALERT: GIANT ROBOT. 366 MAZZUCCHELLI ST.

I blinked, wondering if I'd just read that wrong. It was dark, we were being tossed around inside a toolshed,

I'd almost died two or three times already—a guy could easily make a mistake looking at an address, you know? I *hoped* I'd read it wrong. But I hadn't, and Max and George hadn't either.

366 MAZZUCCHELLI ST.

"Dude, that's your house," Max said.

CHAPTER

"What . . . why is he going to . . ."

"HEY! HEEEEY! POLLYYYYYYYYY!" I hollered. I tried to turn around and pound on the walls of the toolshed, but one of my feet got snarled up with one of George's feet and I ended up smacking Max on the side of the head.

"OW, DUDE!" Max's big gorilla hand grabbed my flailing arm and gently forced it away from his head. "Calm down," he said in what I guess was supposed to be a soothing voice. "Be calm, man, freaking out's not gonna help."

"OH, SHUT UP, YOU DON'T GET TO TELL ME WHAT TO DO! MY HOUSE! WE GOTTA HURRY TO MY HOOOOOUUUUUUSE!"

Max let go of my arm without saying anything.

It's *never* a good thing when a supervillain attacks a

house where regular people live. And I had a terrible feeling Stupendous's no-abduction streak was finally over.

"Why are you getting mad at Max?" George said. He sounded honestly confused, which made me want to punch him in the face. "He's not the one attacking your house."

"George, don't—just drop it," Max said.

"What? I'm just—"

"HEY, STUPENDOUS! HEEEEEYYYYYYY!"

Stupendous must have heard me, because the toolshed lurched, tilted suddenly to about a forty-five degree angle, and stayed that way. Max landed pretty much on top of me, which drove all the air out of my lungs. Was Max wearing cologne? It smelled like he'd just poured a whole bottle over his head. I gasped like a fish out of water as all three of us slid toward the bottom of the shed. It felt like we were moving *fast*.

Aaaaaand *THUNK*, we landed hard. Again. It was almost like Stupendous just tossed the stupid toolshed to the ground, though, because it landed on its side. Naturally the side that was on the ground was the side I was on, so George and I ended up with Max on top of both of us.

Stupendous yanked the door completely off the toolshed with a plasticky *CRUNCH*, tossed it to the side, and looked inside.

"What's with all the screaming in there?" he said.

"Rough landing," George said, with a groan.

"I had to come in fast, otherwise all those people down the hill would have seen us."

"MY HOUSE!" I yelled.

"Vincent, I know this is freaky, but somebody's gonna hear you," Max said. "And then they'll see us up here with Captain Stupendous."

"Yeah, keep it down, Vincent," Stupendous said.

I tried to push Max off me but he was too heavy, so I waited until he got up (digging his heel really hard into my shin in the process) and climbed out, then pulled myself out, using the edge of the doorway. George did the same on the other side. We were in Skyside Park, which is on the hill overlooking my backyard. It's the highest point in our neighborhood, but the middle of the hill is totally covered with eucalyptus trees. It's probably the best superhero landing spot that's also anywhere close to my house. You can look through the eucalyptus trees right at my house without being seen.

I got right up to the inner edge of the eucalyptus patch and peeked out from behind a tree, and, yep, I could see my house. Especially the giant hole in the roof. The cops and other people swarming around it were pretty hard to miss too.

"Oh man," Max said in a soft voice.

I heard Stupendous say "stupendify" somewhere behind me, then Polly and George crept up behind the outermost trees and peeked out too.

DING, DING, DING! It took me a minute, but I at last saw the pattern. I'd thought of the attack on Spud's as being in *my* neighborhood, and the weird inspection of the school district building as a totally random thing, but finally I got it.

Spud's Pizza: my *mom's* neighborhood. The school district offices: my *mom's* work. My house: my *mom's* house. Professor Mayhem was after my mom!

And it looked like he got her.

"You guys, Professor Mayhem's after my MOM! When he fought Stupendous at Spud's, he was probably on his way to our house, and during the second fight he wasn't looking for money, he was looking for my mom's office!"

"Huh." George scratched his head. "Because she's the school superintendent? Really?"

"How am I supposed to know WHY?"

"Maybe she wasn't home?" Polly said.

I pointed at the driveway.

"That's her car."

I actually felt cold, which was one of those things I thought only happened in movies. Then I felt weird and bad for thinking about movies when it was pretty clear my mom had just been kidnapped. Then I felt cold again. Maybe my brain was on the fritz—doesn't shock make stuff like that happen?

"Vincent, don't—"

I was so spaced out I couldn't even tell who was talking—it could have been Max, could have been Polly, could have been an intelligent squirrel. It didn't matter anyway, because I took off running down the hill.

"Vincent! Wait for us!"

I think that's the fastest I've ever run—it's a miracle I didn't wipe out on my way down the hill, which is really steep. Not even George kept up with me. I couldn't tell if the pounding in my ears was the sound of my feet or the sound of my heartbeat, but it was loud. By the time I reached my block I wasn't hearing anything else, so when Bobby caught me in a bear hug as I ran toward the house, it was a complete surprise.

"—OP, VINCENT, STOP!" he shouted as I collided with him at top speed. "You need to stay out here with me, okay?"

I stared past him at the house, which could have been a set for an action movie, what with the hole in the roof and the giant robot footprints in the lawn.

"OKAY?" Bobby said again. He didn't yell, exactly, but

his voice was still really loud. He grabbed my shoulders, turned me around, and tried to look me in the eye, but I kept trying to look behind me at the house.

"Mom," I said in a small voice.

"We're on it, Vincent. We'll get her back, but right now we need to get you to safety."

"Get her back . . . safety . . . wait, what do you mean?" I pulled back from Bobby, but he kept a solid grip on my shoulders.

"We're taking you to your father, Vincent, at Corwin Towers. They have the best security in the city. You'll be safe from Professor Mayhem there."

"No, no, no, Captain Stupendous . . . he has to—"

"Captain Stupendous isn't here." I actually stopped trying to see the house and looked right at Bobby when I heard that. He sounded seriously bummed out, and kinda mad. "We're handling this one ourselves, and we need to get you to a safe location, just in case Professor Mayhem comes back. Come on."

"Wait, wait, wait, Bobby, WAIT!"

Bobby didn't wait, though. He just hustled me over to a nearby police car, said, "Watch your head," and pretty much stuffed me into the backseat.

"Go!" he barked at the driver.

I looked wildly around for Polly and the guys, and I

spotted them at the edge of the crowd, behind one of those sawhorse barrier things the cops use to separate you from your friends when you really need them. I couldn't hear but I could see Polly yelling at the cops who were keeping her behind the barrier. She had her fists clenched and her arms stuck out completely straight, and her glossy black hair flipped back and forth as she yelled. Another cop was physically holding George as he kicked and twisted. The cop had a handful of George's shirt, which was pulled up far enough to show George's entire stomach. Max, on the other hand, was looking down. As the cop in front of me started the engine, Max bent down slowly, like a ballet dancer with giant shoulders, then stood back up, holding something. It looked like a leaf, or maybe a feather.

The cop car screeched into motion. Two more cop cars pulled out on either side of us, and with sirens blaring and lights flashing, the cops took me away.

CHAPTER

Bobby didn't mess around with my police escort—there was the police car I rode in with two cops, two extra cars driving ahead and behind us, each with two more cops, and I'm pretty sure there was a helicopter flying above us, probably with eleven cops armed with rocket launchers. It was freaky, but it was also the first time ever that Captain Stupendous didn't even show up for a battle.

Which was my fault, when I thought about it.

I was about ready to start punching myself in the face and never stop when we reached Corwin Towers, right in the heart of downtown Copperplate City. Normally I make a point of looking around down there, because there's some cool stuff in that part of town, but I was too distracted by the panicky voice yelling, "GAH! GAH! GAH!" in my brain to pay much attention. Next thing I knew, we'd circled the block and driven right into a very brightly lit underground parking garage.

The top level of the garage was full of cars, but then we hit a spiral ramp that went down to a level that was smaller, and full of big, dark, four-door cars that looked like they should be driven by secret agents. There was a bank of elevators at one end of the garage level, and as the cops let me out of the car, one of the elevator doors opened. Out came a bunch of guys in dark suits and headsets, a couple of cops, and my dad.

"Vincent!" Dad must have been as freaked out as I was because he dropped his usual absentminded-professor thing and actually *ran* over. He pushed his glasses (which had slipped down his nose) all the way back onto his face with his left middle finger and grabbed me. One of the buttons on his shirt dug into my chin, and he smelled a little bit sweaty. I'm not the hugging type, just so you know— usually when I hug Dad it's only to make *him* happy—but I have to admit, I felt better when he hugged me really tightly.

"I saw you on TV the other day," I blurted out for no reason.

"The Kobayashi press conference, eh?" Dad held me at arm's length, one hand behind my shoulder and the other hand behind my head. "I was terrified that you were at the house when that lunatic attacked, Vincent. I'm so glad you're all right."

"Have you . . ." Geez, I didn't even know what to ask first, because most of what I wanted to ask I *couldn't* ask—was it crazy to think I could help Polly learn how to be Captain Stupendous? What would happen if she didn't figure it out? *Was it my fault Mom got kidnapped?* "Have you heard anything about Mom? And do they know who Professor Mayhem *is?*"

Dad shook his head, which made his hair fall across his forehead. There were maybe a dozen white hairs scattered around on Dad's head—they looked almost shiny compared to all the black hairs around them. He rubbed his forehead with the palm of his hand, fingers spread open. "Nobody knows anything yet."

"Dr. Wu, we should get you into the fully secure area of the building," one of the dark-suited guys with the headsets said. His voice was very deep. "Ms. Corwin insists."

We went back into the elevator with the Corwin security people and the two cops who'd come down with them. We were on level S2, which I guessed was still underground because there were other buttons above it that said S1, G4–G1, B, L, and *then* numbers from 1 to 100.

"Big building, huh?" Dad said. "Don't worry, we're not staying in the underground levels—we won't have any windows, though. We'll be in the very middle of the towers."

"Dad . . . Professor Mayhem's got—"

"I know, Vincent." Dad put his arm around me. "I *know*. But the police seem to think we're in danger, and they're probably right. We'll be safe here."

"*Mom's* not safe." *And Stupendous is a girl! And I'm stuck in here without my friends! And Mom's been abducted by a supervillain!*

I mean, I was glad Mayhem didn't kidnap my dad too, but suddenly it felt like the whole world had turned to garbage, you know?

The elevator let us out into a wide hallway with deep blue carpet on the floor, huge framed pictures of buildings all up and down the walls, and a series of big windows to our right. After a few hundred feet we went through a door on the left, down another long hallway, and into a room with a whole mess of security guys standing outside the door. The room had no windows, but there was a couch against one wall, a gigantic TV screen on the opposite wall, and at least four big leather chairs and coffee tables. There were doors on either side of the couch, and through one of them I could see the edge of a bed.

"So what, Dad, are we supposed to *live* here until somebody rescues Mom?"

"That's the idea. I don't like it any more than you do."

"But . . . but . . ."

AAAGH! Secrets! I couldn't tell Dad about Polly and Captain Stupendous! Stupid secret identities and other secret stuff!

"But what if we can do something, Dad?" I threw myself full length on the couch and let one arm and leg hang off the front of the cushions. "What if we can help?"

"Vincent, there's nothing we can do." I was flopped over the whole middle of the couch, but it was big enough for Dad to sit next to me without sitting on my head. "I wish we could."

"Bobby's helping." I felt a streak of anger go through me when I said it. I also felt Dad twitch, which made me feel a little bad, but then I felt mad again. *Bobby's not hiding!*

"Bobby's a police officer, Vincent." Dad's voice was monotone. His face looked almost expressionless, except for the way his jaw muscles slowly clenched and unclenched. He closed his eyes for a few seconds, then blinked once, hard.

"I know, Vincent. I'm worried about your mom too, you know." Dad patted me on the shoulder, then rubbed his own head, still with that almost-no-expression expression on his face. "But I—"

The door we'd come in opened, and a security guy stuck his head in.

"Dr. Wu, you should turn on the TV," he said.

Dad and I looked at each other, then he jumped up as I scrambled to my feet. Dad grabbed the biggest remote control I'd ever seen off a coffee table and turned on the TV, which was already on the Corwin Network.

We caught about a half second of Patty Suarez saying, "—ive broadcast of suspe—" before the screen went black, then cut to a shot of an old man behind a desk. He was dressed all in red—red shirt, red lab coat, and red gloves. He had a pair of big red goggles shoved up on his head and one elbow on the desk, with two fingers propped against his forehead. The other hand did a *rat-a-tat-tat* drumming thing on the table. His eyebrows were like huge, bristly centipedes.

"Thank you, Ms. Suarez, but I believe I'd like to reveal that tidbit myself," he said in a slow, deep voice. His fingers kept drumming on the table, *THWIDIDIDUMP. THWIDIDIDUMP.*

"I am Professor Mayhem."

Dad dropped the remote control on the carpet with a muffled *THUNK.*

"Oh no," he said. "This is NOT possible."

"What? What is it?"

"It can't be him." Dad was clenching his fists. Actually, no, it was more like he was grinding his fingernails into

the palms of his hands, and his mouth was open in a toothy snarl. Holy cow. Dad was *pissed off*!

"WHAT IS IT, DAD?"

Dad held up a finger, waved it around next to his ear like a gun, then pointed at the TV in a jerky motion.

"I know him! *I went to high school with that idiot!*"

For a second I was confused, because it was like Dad transmogrified into a different version of himself—more slouchy, a little bit of a whinier voice, maybe even shorter? It was bizarre, like he was channeling his inner teenager.

"Professor Mayhem my eye, that's plain old Dennis Mayhem!" Dad ran his hands through his hair, then laced them behind his neck.

"You *know* him? Seriously?"

"I haven't seen that misanthropic pig face in twenty-five years, not since—"

I kinda wanted to know since when, but Dad stopped talking when Professor Mayhem started.

"Greetings, citizens of Copperplate City," Professor Mayhem said. "So pleased to make your acquaintance."

The door opened again and a whole crowd of people came in, and not just security guys this time (although there were a few of them too). There was an old lady, a couple of guys in jeans and hoodies, a woman in a lab coat, and . . . Bobby? Yep, it was Bobby, with two of his cop buddies.

The old lady came and stood next to Dad, and everybody else gathered around the TV as Professor Mayhem went on.

"It appears I have your miserable little city to myself, worms. Unless Captain Stupendous chooses to show his face momentarily?"

Mayhem stuck one hand behind his ear, being all exaggerated about it, and pretended to listen.

"No, it appears not! Excellent. Let's get down to the meat of it, shall we? By now even a gaggle of simpletons like you all realize I've stolen away your superintendent of schools, my old paramour Violet Keller."

Mom!

"PARAMOUR?" Dad yelled at the TV in such a psychotic voice that I jumped and waved my arms around like Max. "SHE WAS NEVER YOUR PARAMOUR, YOU TROGLODYTE!"

"A charming lass, with whom I'm delighted to renew my relationship." Professor Mayhem looked like he was having a good time—he grinned, drummed his fingers on the table, and wiggled his dead-caterpillar eyebrows.

"But of course she's not the only one I'm here to see. Ray-Ray? Are you out there, my old foe? I imagine you're cowering in some inadequately defended rodent run inside Corwin Towers, eh?"

Huh. Good guess.

"*Ray-Ray?*" the old lady said. "Oh my stars, Raymond, is that cretin talking to *you*?"

Dad ground his teeth together.

"It's a long story, Janet," he said.

"What a tragic ending to your storybook romance, Ray-Ray!" Mayhem giggled, which was maybe the creepiest sound I'd ever heard. "I trust you won't stand in the way if Violet and I pick up where we left off? But perhaps we should talk it over first, being the gentlemen we are."

He grinned again, with his lips pulled so far back from his teeth that you could see his top AND bottom gums. Gross.

"In fact, Ray-Ray, I *insist* we talk it over. Here at my headquarters—I'll even provide transportation! Meet me at Corwin Stadium tomorrow at noon. Perhaps that coward Captain Stupendous will even join us, eh? Oh, and in case you also succumb to cowardice, I'll provide a bit of incentive."

Mayhem slammed both hands down on the table in front of him and glared out from the screen, not smiling at all anymore.

"I'm fond of Violet, Ray-Ray—she's still quite the scrumptious little bird—but if you fail to appear tomorrow, I won't hesitate to kill her."

CHAPTER

Ever feel like your senses have suddenly gone screwy and stopped working right? That's how I felt when I heard Mayhem say he'd kill Mom—everything looked kinda foggy, all the objects in the room looked like they were a little bit farther away than before, and there was a funny whooshing sound in my ears. After a little bit I realized somebody was calling my name.

"—incent! Vincent! VINCENT!"

My head waggled back and forth as Dad shook me.

"Vincent! Are you all right?"

"Blergh," I said. "I mean, yeah . . . no . . . I don't know. Is Captain Stupendous out there looking for Mom?"

"I don't know." Dad looked at Bobby, who shook his head.

"No sign of him, I'm afraid, but we're doing everything we can to get your mom back."

Crap! Where were Polly and the guys? Why weren't they DOING something? Or did they try to stop Professor Mayhem and get taken out? Were they even alive?

I had to get out of Corwin Towers and find out! *Mom!*

"Dr. Wu." Bobby turned to my dad, looking grim. "We have some decisions to make, but first we should gather any information you have about Professor Mayhem."

"Of course," Dad said. "I'll . . . I'll do anything I can to help Violet."

Dad had his arm around my shoulders, so I could feel him shaking. Was he scared? Bobby didn't look scared—he stood up so straight a flagpole would have looked crooked in comparison. I didn't see even one wrinkle in his uniform. He looked ready to leap into action.

"What are you gonna do?" I asked him.

"I don't know about you strapping young men, but these old bones need a place to sit down," the old lady said. She gave Dad and me a genteel shove in the direction of the couch. It wasn't a really hard shove, but Dad moved toward the couch anyway.

"You know Professor Mayhem," Bobby said. The way he said it was like half question, half regular sentence. He pulled some kind of digital recorder thingy out of his pocket, pushed a button, and put it on the table in front of Dad.

"His real name is Dennis Mayhem," Dad said, sounding more like his normal self. "We went to high school together at Xavier High, over in the Gaslamp District. I haven't seen him in almost twenty-five years."

"It sounds like you knew him pretty well, if you both dated Violet." Bobby didn't sound calm, exactly, but he sounded in control. His voice was firm, and his hands weren't shaking like Dad's. And he didn't look mad, exactly, but there was one long furrow on his face—it started right at the inside tip of his right eyebrow and went halfway up his forehead.

Dad snorted. His glasses slid an inch or two down his nose.

"Dennis never dated Violet," he said, and snorted again. He pushed his glasses back up with his thumb. "He *wished* he could have dated her, but she never gave him a second look. Violet was with *me*."

"So he considered you a . . . romantic rival?"

"I suppose, but it was academically that we were genuine rivals. We were both . . . we were both science geeks, you could probably say. We were both interested in what they called earth science back then."

Dad was a science geek in high school—not exactly a shock. The fact that he was enemies with a future supervillain? Huge, massive, mind-blowing shock. Throw in the fact that the future supervillain had a thing for Mom and, dude, it was like my parents used to be, you know, *young.*

"Xavier High had a very good chem lab for advanced students back then, and Dennis and I both made full use of it. We competed in a lot of ways—I won the state science fair three years in a row, for example. And after junior year I was accepted by the Takahashi Global Consortium's summer research program, which rejected him."

"Did he have a scientific specialty?"

"Do we have time for this?" I couldn't keep it in—as interesting as it was to hear about Dad's high school dork war with Dennis Mayhem, I was practically chewing my arm off to help Stupendous find Mom. Of course I had to find Stupendous first. Crapola! I stood up and started walking in circles.

"I know this is hard, Vincent," Bobby said. He leaned out in front of me, which stopped me from pacing, and looked right into my eyes. "This is harder on you than anybody, but believe me, I'm worried about your mom too. I don't think Professor Mayhem will hurt her until his deadline—villains almost never do that."

"Lizardlips did it." I stopped and put my hands on top of my head.

"Lizardlips was a completely alien life-form," Bobby said. "With a strange diet. Professor Mayhem is human, which makes him . . . not predictable, maybe, but not completely unpredictable. Your mother will be safe tonight. Okay?"

I scratched the top of my head with both hands. Hard. "OKAY?"

"Yeah, yeah, okay, okay." I flopped down on the couch next to Dad, who put an arm around my bony shoulders.

"We'll get her back, Vincent," Dad said. "I don't know how, but we'll get her back."

I muttered under my breath—no words, just muttering.

"Dr. Wu, I know these questions may seem pointless, but I'm just hunting for any possible weaknesses," Bobby said. "Did Dennis Mayhem have a particular scientific specialty?"

Dad sat with his head bowed, thinking. "He was—is, I suppose—a genuine polymath, Detective. He was interested in many, many things. But I always wondered if he'd pursue metallurgy of some kind, particularly after we found . . ."

"We?" I said. "Like, you and him?"

"What did you find, Dr. Wu?"

Dad took a deep breath and closed his eyes, but just for a second. "Detective, I don't know how old you are, but you look to be in shouting distance of my age—you're from Gigawatt City, correct?"

"No, sir, I lived there for a number of years but I'm from Copperplate City, born and bred. I went to Ororo Munroe High."

Dad cracked a brief smile. "Go Storms, eh?"

"Yes, sir, thunder and lightning. I played linebacker."

"Well, that fits, then, doesn't it? You must remember that remarkable meteor shower we had twenty-six years ago."

Bobby nodded. "Yes. The papers were full of stories about UFOs."

I was getting more and more freaked out about Mom, but I also wanted to hear more. Dad talked about it like it was some old-school childhood memory, but that summer's meteor shower is *legendary* among Captain Stupendous fans. Bobby must have guessed what I was thinking, because he gave me a quick, tiny smile.

"Vincent, if that look on your face is any indication, you know something about that meteor shower," he said.

"Yeah. A lot of people think Captain Stupendous first got his powers that summer—maybe even from a UFO. The *Copperplate Chronicle* ran a bunch of articles on it, the library has them all on file."

Dad nodded and looked at me with one eyebrow raised.

"What?" A little grenade of anger went off in my stomach. "You didn't think I'd know about that, Dad?"

Dad opened his mouth for a second, closed it, then opened it again. "Well, I just . . . it was . . . it happened a long time ago. I didn't think you were interested in history."

"Knowing about Captain Stupendous IS knowing about history!"

"Point taken." Dad started talking, but this time he looked at me instead of Bobby.

"I was hanging around at Skyside Park one day— Dennis was there too, although he was off by himself.

There were only one or two other people there, though. Most kids went to Lake Higgleman to socialize."

"Aw, gross," I said.

"The lake was nicer back then, Vincent," Bobby said. "In those days there weren't *any* geese living there—the lake was the hip place to be."

"Right," Dad said. "The hip place. So, not many people were there to see the meteorites fall to earth."

"You *saw* them?" Bobby said, and for just a second he didn't look worried or businesslike or any of that stuff. His eyes got round, and he shifted his weight up to the front of his chair.

"More than that," Dad said. "I *found* one, and so did Dennis. Three meteorites landed in all—Miguel Zazueta was actually hit by the third one."

I totally jumped up out of my chair.

"MR. ZAZUETA? IS THAT HOW—" I clamped both hands over my mouth, which probably didn't make me look any less suspicious. Lucky for me, Dad misunderstood.

"I don't know if it caused him long-term health problems, but it's not why he died," Dad said. "He had a heart attack. But he did go to the hospital after the meteorite hit him. Some kids started a rumor that he'd been abducted by a UFO, but nobody took it seriously."

"There were a lot of alien abduction claims that summer," Bobby said. "They're on record in the police archives."

My head was spinning. *That's how it must have happened! Aliens! Aliens made Captain Stupendous!*

Of course, me knowing that didn't help Mom at all, and that thought made my head spin in the opposite direction. It must have, because I felt like I might start throwing up and never stop. I wondered if everyone who had their mom kidnapped by a supervillain felt the same way.

"The meteorite I picked up was just a rubbery lump, but it turned out to be an incredibly complex polycarbon. It took me two decades to decode its molecular structure and replicate it."

"Carbon nanotube monofilaments," Bobby said, and smiled. "I've read a little about your work."

"Yes. That meteorite has been the foundation of my entire career."

The digital recorder on the table beeped.

"Excuse me," Bobby said. He picked up the recorder, pressed a couple of buttons, and put it back on the table. Doing that seemed to put Bobby back in 100 percent businesslike cop mode.

"What did Dennis Mayhem find?" Just the way he asked the question made me want to tell him the right answer, but Dad shook his head.

"I don't know," Dad said. "By that point he'd developed an infatuation with Violet. It became disturbing quickly: He started following her around in the halls, attending all of the women's volleyball games, and so on. He couldn't stand it that I was with her. We weren't capable of being civil with each other, so we kept our distance. I saw him pick something out of a meteorite crater, but I didn't see what it was. He's clearly mastered robotics, however, so I'd guess it was an unknown ore mineral.

"That was the last time I'd seen him. Until today."

There was a knock on the door, and this time a cop stuck his head inside.

"Uh, Detective? Someone's here."

"For me?" Bobby started to get up, but the other cop shook his head and pointed with his thumb.

"No, for *him*." He was pointing at me!

The cop's head disappeared, the door opened all the way, and in walked Captain Stupendous.

CHAPTER

At first I had my usual, automatic Yippee-Captain-Stupendous-to-the-rescue! reaction to seeing him. I felt a serious rush, you know? Then I remembered what the real deal was, and it was like somebody yanked my power cord out of the wall.

The way Stupendous acted didn't help. He stopped a couple of steps inside the door when he saw all the people in the room. He stood there with his shoulders slightly hunched and his arms stuck straight out, angled away from his body, and both hands in fists. I felt my whole body clench a little bit more just from looking at him. He looked at me and tilted his head a tiny bit while opening his eyes really wide. I hate it when people do the body-language thing; I can never tell what they're trying to say.

Bobby broke the silence by offering a hand to Stupendous.

"Captain Stupendous, it's an honor to meet you," he said. "I'm Detective Bobby Carpenter."

Stupendous stared at Bobby's hand, then wrapped his arms around himself and scratched the top of one foot with the toes on his other foot.

Bobby never changed expression, but I saw Dad's eyebrows go up, and one of the security guys turned and looked at one of the other security guys, who gave a tiny shrug.

Finally Stupendous shook Bobby's hand. Bobby pumped hands twice and let go, and Stupendous lifted that hand and ran it through his hair.

"This is Dr. Ray Wu, and it sounds like you, ah, already know Vincent?"

"Hey." Stupendous nodded in Dad's direction. "Right. I mean, yeah, I know Vincent."

"You *know* my son?" Dad's eyes looked like they were about to pop out of his head.

"I assume you're informed about the Violet Keller abduction?" Bobby looked and sounded totally confident that Stupendous would say yes.

"Who?"

Bobby's expression still didn't change, but he stared at Stupendous for a few seconds. Dad, on the other hand, looked like he was about to cough up a lung.

"I was, you know, on my way here," Stupendous said. He shifted his weight from one leg to the other. "To talk to Vincent."

Everybody turned to look at me. The security guys made me feel especially creeped out, especially the one who was wearing his stupid mirrored shades inside.

"Um . . . err, yeah, we're gonna go . . . in there." And I pointed to one of the bedroom doors.

I turned and walked into the bedroom without waiting. Stupendous came in and shut the door behind me, and I spun around.

"YOU DON'T KNOW—" I started, but Stupendous shushed me with a finger in front of his mouth.

"Not so loud!" he said in a loud whisper.

"You *don't know* about Professor Mayhem and my mom?" I said in a lower voice.

"Like, hello? Thanks for coming to rescue me?" Stupendous crossed his arms and stood with one hip stuck out to the side.

"Who cares about hello? Professor Mayhem is gonna kill my mom!"

"What?"

I gave him the rundown on Mayhem's TV broadcast.

". . . so he's gonna kill her if Dad doesn't show up and turn himself in tomorrow at the stadium."

"Oh. Oh geez, Vincent." Stupendous put his hands over his mouth. He walked over and sat on the bed.

"Will he really do it?"

I shrugged. "I don't wanna find out. You have to locate Mayhem's headquarters and get her out of there."

And that's when I really understood how deep the doo-doo was, because the real, *original* Captain Stupendous could have done that with no problem, right?

Things wouldn't even be this bad in the first place if Mr. Zazueta was still running the show.

And it wouldn't be this bad if it wasn't for my brilliant idea to visit Colossal Dome at the exact time my mom was being kidnapped. Yep, things were completely in the toilet with lame old Vincent Wu trying to run the show.

I put my face in my hands and started crying like the wussy boy I truly was.

"Whoa, hey, Vincent, take it easy," Stupendous said. I heard him jump to his feet, and a second later he petted me on the head like a dog. "It's gonna be okay, I swear."

"HOW'S IT GONNA BE OKAY?" I shouted, not even caring if Dad and Bobby and all the Corwin Towers security people heard me. "HOW? I DON'T KNOW WHERE PROFESSOR MAYHEM'S SECRET HEADQUARTERS IS, DO YOU?"

"Well, actually—"

The door opened and this time it was Dad sticking his head into the room.

"Vincent, are you—"

"GET OUT!" Stupendous hollered, and I knew from experience how hard it is to ignore him when he yells like that. A framed picture fell off the wall, bounced off the bed, and crashed onto the floor. Dad immediately shut the door, probably more from reflexes than anything else.

I glared at Stupendous with his big old muscles and his stupid, weird girl secret identity like I hated him more than anybody else in the world, and he just looked down at the floor.

"Max and George actually do have a theory on where Mayhem's headquarters is."

"They do? Really?" I should have felt . . . I don't know, relieved or hopeful to hear that, but I just felt worse.

"Totally."

"Well, that's perfect. It was my idea to go to Colossal Dome, and that's when Mayhem kidnapped my mom. It's practically my fault she was taken. You should just leave me here, it sounds like you guys are doing fine without me."

"Oh, you've GOT to be kidding me, Vincent." Stupendous frowned. "We *all* went to Colossal Dome."

"Yeah, but it was my idea."

"Well, then, come on, think of another idea to fix it!" Stupendous's eyes started to glow.

"I can't, I'm stuck in the middle of Corwin Towers with a million cops and security people around me."

Stupendous made an *AARHGGLE* sound and looked at the ceiling.

"So you're just quitting, huh?"

"*You're* the superhero! I'm just another scrawny geek in the galaxy's worst superhero fan club."

"He's gonna kill her tomorrow, right?"

"Right." *She's doomed. What can we do? What can I do?*

"Well, you better help me figure out what to do tonight."

Stupendous stood up and cracked his knuckles. I flopped backward on the bed.

"So what, you're gonna bust me out of here?" I said to the ceiling.

With a jerk the ceiling got a lot closer to my face, then I saw the room whirl around me until I was staring over Stupendous's shoulder at the bedroom door.

"Yep, I'm gonna bust you out of here, fan boy. Hang on."

"WHOA, HEY, WHAT ARE YOU—"

Stupendous carried me to the wall opposite the door, and even though I couldn't see, the *BAM* sound and the spray of dust and chunks of plaster made it pretty obvious what he was doing.

Stupendous *was* busting me out, by punching straight through the walls of the building.

CHAPTER

"Wait, why don't we just walk out?" I shouted. I had to shout, because busting through a wall is louder than you might think. It's not just the punching and the walls collapsing, it's also the yelling and the doors slamming and the alarms going off. At least that's what it was like in Corwin Towers.

"You seriously think they're gonna let me just take you to Professor Mayhem's headquarters with me? Ha!" Stupendous shouted as he punched through another wall.

"Hey, hey, wait a minute—*me* go to Mayhem's headquarters? What are you talking abou—"

I was distracted by the pack of security guys we stepped into the middle of after punching through the latest wall.

"Captain Stupendous, cease and desist!" one of them yelled.

"Piss off!" Stupendous yelled back.

"I told him to stop but he wouldn't listen!" I yelled. It just slipped out—it'd been a crazy day, you know? Stupendous looked back at me. I couldn't actually see his face, but I could tell from the shape of his cheeks that he was grinning.

"You are such a goody two-shoes," he said. "No wonder Mrs. Burnell likes you so much, you're a total teacher's pet."

"I am not a teach—AAAACKK . . ." *BAM!* A torn strip of wallpaper smacked me in the face as Stupendous bashed his way out into that wide hallway with the windows, which I guess went all the way around the building. There were a bunch of people in work clothes walking around, and they stopped and dropped their papers and briefcases and stuff when we came through the wall.

"Captain Stupendous!" a girl in a black shirt and skirt said, gawking at us. She smiled and smoothed out her hair as a bunch of security guys appeared around her.

"Later, posers," Stupendous said. He looked around and spotted a hideous metal statue of a man (or maybe it was a woman, it was hard to tell) with really long, thin arms and legs and a lumpy watermelon of a head. The statue was set on a big black pedestal with a velvet rope around it. Stupendous grabbed the statue, yanked it off the pedestal, and hoisted it like a javelin.

"WAIT, ARE YOU GONNA THROW THAT?" I shouted. "NO, YOU'LL—"

"Calm down, Vincent," Stupendous said. His arm bunched up—I swear, his shoulder muscle alone was bigger than the entire top half of my body—and threw the statue.

"MOVE, MOVE, MOVE!" I made hyperactive sweeping motions with my arms, which may have been a waste of time since Stupendous was facing the windows, which meant I was facing the hole we'd just made in the wall. "GET AWAY FROM THE WINDOWS!"

KERRAAAAASH! I heard the window shatter, then *BAZOOM*, my head snapped back and my arms were flung out parallel to Stupendous's body as we took off. I briefly saw a crowd of people staring out the bashed-open window of Corwin Towers, but we pulled away fast—the busted window, the whole side of the building, the whole tower, the downtown skyline, then we were in the night sky.

"It got dark," I said, feeling like a total space case. I couldn't think of anything else to say, though, and I was distracted by my hair—the wind was blowing it around in all directions. It was like having a cloud of hair descend on my forehead.

"Yeah," Stupendous said. "By the way, the cops are still all over your house, so we're going to MY house."

I had a crazy vision of flying into the rumored-to-be-amazing secret headquarters of Captain Stupendous, then I snapped back to my senses. *Polly's* house. Would we make our rescue plans in Polly's room? I'd never been in a girl's room before, unless you count my cousin Jennifer.

In the dark it was hard to tell what part of the city we were flying over, but after a few minutes I saw lit-up swimming pools and big, big houses. The pools were like shiny blue kidney beans, floating in the dark, and the houses were far apart. There were two rows of tiny lights leading up to each house—driveways, probably.

We stopped over one of the biggest houses in the whole neighborhood—there was actually a garden on the *roof.* The kidney-shaped swimming pool looked like a killer whale could comfortably live in it, and there was a little house to one side, probably for changing into swimsuits or something like that. We dropped fast into the yard.

"Home sweet home—hang on a second," Stupendous said. He ducked into the changing house, and I saw a quick flash of blue light from under the door. A second later Polly stepped out.

"Listen, my parents are out of town, but our housekeeper, Annabelle, is here, so we have to be quiet when we go in, got it?" she said.

"Sure." I looked around the yard, which was filled with

patio furniture and had a mammoth brick oven over by the actual house. A bunch of metal tables and chairs were spread out around it, and the lawn went on for miles. The yard by itself was probably bigger than the whole block I lived on.

"So . . . you're rich, huh?" I said as we snuck across the yard.

"No, my parents are," Polly said. "Keep it down, will you?"

There was a set of big sliding glass doors right in the center of the house, but Polly went to a regular door around the corner, unlocked it, and eased it open. The house seemed even bigger on the inside—we tiptoed through a kitchen the size of an airport, with steel and polished rock surfaces everywhere, then up a flight of stairs that was wide enough for at least six people to walk side by side. At the foot of the stairs I heard a TV somewhere close by.

"Hey, Annabelle," Polly called in the direction of the TV, not bothering to stop moving. She did a come-on gesture with her hand, palm up and fingers flapping, as the not-visible Annabelle said, "hi, Polly" in a faint voice. We took the stairs to the second floor, then down a dark hallway.

I guess my impression of girl bedrooms was based completely on my cousin Jennifer's room, which is so pink and full of foofy ruffled blankets and rhinestones that you want to scream. Polly's room? NOT foofy. The place was covered in concert posters for weirdo bands I'd never heard of—Lizard Brain, The Wire and the Fire, Mock Apple Pie—and a guitar covered with stickers was propped up in the far corner of the room. The walls were painted dark red, but I wouldn't have been surprised if they'd been painted black. There were no stuffed animals in sight. There *was* a really big set of closet doors, though, and after a few seconds one of them slid open and Max and George climbed out of it.

"Dude, finally," George said.

"Yeah, we were wondering if you were ever gonna make it." Max punched me on the shoulder—not too hard—and grinned at Polly. Which made no sense at all, since I was the one who'd been hauled off by the cops. "You have the craziest wardrobe, Polly. I've never seen so many puffy dresses in one place before."

"Blame my mom," Polly said. "The only reason I don't light 'em all on fire is because I know she'll go ballistic."

"Want a muffin, Vincent?" George held up a half-full basket of them. "Lemon and poppy seed, they're good."

I looked at Polly, who shrugged. "All we have in the kitchen is leftover Thai food and muffins. Annabelle makes them."

"Thanks." I took two and bit the entire top off one. I held up a finger and chewed furiously, then swallowed. The lump of chewed muffin barely made it through.

"Any new news about my mom?"

"Nothing yet, but we're keeping an eye on the news," Max said. He pointed at Polly's TV, which took up about three-quarters of the wall across from her bed. "Sorry, dude. We gotta get her back."

"No kidding, but how are *we* gonna do that, Max?" Suddenly I felt so, so, so tired. I sat on Polly's bed, then flopped onto my back and stared at the ceiling.

"Are you asking me?" Max pointed at his own chest, right at the spot where his T-shirt stretched between his pecs.

"Yeah."

"Nobody ever asks me," George mumbled.

"What?" Polly squinted at George.

"Nothing, nothing."

Polly's room had the nicest ceiling fan I'd ever seen— the fan blades were light-colored wood with a cool, swirly pattern in the grain. Two chains hung down from it, one hanging lower than the other, and the little handles on the ends of them looked like they were made out of marble.

"What happened to 'oh Max, you're too bossy' and all that?" Max's eyebrows were knotted together, but not in a mad way, more like a confused way.

"Look where my ideas got us. Kidnapped, locked up, hiding in a girl's closet . . . I probably *shouldn't* be president of the club."

"Oh come on, Vincent, knock it off," Polly said.

"Seriously," I said. "I'm done. Besides, Polly says you guys figured out where Mayhem is without me, right?"

"Yeah, we did," Max said slowly.

"Well, spit it out," I said.

"Vincent," George said, with a frown. "Why are—"

"GEORGE," Max said in his I'm-warning-you voice, but George cut him off.

"No, I'm not gonna say something bad, just . . . dude, you're our friend."

"Yeah, big deal," I said.

"Shut up, it IS a big deal!" George barked. "It SUCKED having you locked up, it was even worse than when Max joined the football team!"

Max and I looked at each other and burst out laughing. A second later George joined in.

"Worse than the football team!" I howled.

"I don't know, man, football was pretty bad," Max said, hooting and snorting.

There was a noise downstairs, and Polly furiously shushed us as she dashed over to the door.

"Polly? You okay?" I could barely make out what

Annabelle said from wherever she was. Polly opened the door far enough to stick her head out.

"Fine! Sorry, I'll turn down the volume!"

She closed the door and gave us the stink eye.

"You know, all this male bonding is awesome, but I'm not allowed to have boys up here, so you guys have to keep it down."

Max ignored Polly (for once) and grinned at George.

"Vincent, did you see George trying to get past the police barricade when they took you away?" he said.

I nodded. George's face turned red.

"Did you know George elbowed a cop in the face?"

"Seriously?" I hoisted myself up on my elbows and stared at George with my mouth open. "You? George Loney, law enforcement fan boy, *hitting a cop*?"

George lifted his chin and stuck his chest out a little.

"It was an accident," he said in a prissy voice, kind of like Vice Principal Castle.

"It was *fantastic*," Max said, with an ear-to-ear grin.

"I missed it," Polly said.

"Well, yeah, you were too busy calling the cops every four-letter word in existence," George said, with his own ear-to-ear grin.

"Which was just as fantastic," Max said.

"Aw, you guys totally love me," I said.

"Oh gross, don't make me elbow *you* in the face," George said, but he was obviously trying not to keep smiling.

Polly stuck a finger in her mouth and made gagging noises, but she was smiling a little bit too.

"Why don't you guys just sing 'Kumbaya' and tell Vincent where Mayhem is?" she said, crossing her arms.

"Yeah, spill it," I said.

Max held up a long, brown, wet-looking feather, and when the smell hit me I figured it out too. It was totally obvious, in fact.

"Where's the stinkiest place you've ever been?" George said.

"He's at Lake Higgleman!"

CHAPTER

Everyone was totally exhausted, and after a couple of hours talking about what to do we all fell asleep on the floor of Polly's room without really meaning to. A few hours later I woke up to the sound of somebody saying "psssssst!" in my ear.

"Huh? Whuzzat?" I grunted. I opened my eyes to see Polly looking down at me, holding a finger in front of her mouth.

"Wake up, Vincent, we need to get out there while it's still dark. Don't wake up Annabelle!" Polly stood up and poked Max in the side with her foot, not gently, then did the same to George.

After a totally unsatisfying breakfast of stale muffins we headed out to the lake. We arrived before sunrise, where we learned that the only thing worse than being at Lake Higgleman during the day was being there when it was dark. It smelled just as bad, and you couldn't see any of the goose turds. At least the geese weren't swarming around, looking like they were about to attack you—they were out there in the dark somewhere, maybe just floating on the surface of the lake. I thought about Mom being held prisoner by a supervillain somewhere at the bottom of the lake, and had a quiet freak-out moment.

"So, dude," Max said in a low voice. "Are you . . ." We were at the very edge of the grass, about twenty feet from the edge of the water. Between the grass and the water was mud, mud, more mud, and a zillion cigar-shaped bird turds. We had flashlights, but there were no streetlights or anything out by the lake, so anything that wasn't in the beam of our flashlights was totally black.

"Not so much."

"I figured."

"I guess we should have come up with an actual rescue plan before coming out here, huh?"

"It's gotta be in the water, right?" George said. "It'd be too easy to find if it was out here on land."

"No doubt," I said. "You're just gonna have to look around, you know, in there."

I said that last part to Polly.

"You mean under the water?" It was hard to see her face in the dark, but it looked like she made an *eww* face.

"Ugh. This water's gross enough to kill even a superhero."

"Why are you not in Captain Stupendous form?" George said. "Seriously, we're practically on the front porch of a supervillain."

"Yeah, yeah," Polly said. "I'll do it when I'm ready."

"Hang on, let's just look around the edge of the lake for a little bit," I said. "There might at least be some clue about WHERE in the water Mayhem's headquarters is."

We walked slowly around the edge of the lake, shining our flashlights onto the muddy lakeshore. There were a lot of geese with their heads tucked under their wings, looking like dark, egg-shaped lumps in the mud, but no giant robot footprints or anything like that. There was a *lot* of bug noise, though—chirping, buzzing, whirring, it was like a freaking bug convention.

A quarter of the way around the lake we reached a spot with much taller trees—they were really gigantic, as tall as apartment buildings. Nobody was really talking anymore, we were all just grunting at each other. A trickle of sweat ran behind my ear and down into my shirt. Max and George wandered a little ways into the trees, and Polly and I stood there and looked at each other without saying anything. I cleared my throat and she scratched behind her ear. A bird went *CAW* as it flew overhead, making us both jump. Once I read this book where the characters kept falling into "comfortable silences," which is completely bogus. Silences are always heinous and weird.

"It's just—" Polly blurted out, then stopped. What was she talking about?

"It's just what?" I said.

"It's just that it's messed up, turning into a grown-up, you know?"

Oh. Turning into Stupendous.

"I guess. Is it kind of cool too, though?"

"I don't know, I guess so."

"As Captain Stupendous, you could tell people to do stuff for you and they'd probably just do it."

"Grown-ups don't do *anything* I ask when I'm my regular self. All they do is *tell* me what to do."

"It sucks being a kid. It must be even worse being a girl."

SMACK! "OW!"

Polly must have hit me in the arm with some kind of kung fu death blow—I didn't even see it coming.

"What'd you do that for?" I said.

Polly glared at me with an expression that perfectly matched her death blow.

"Because you're a moron who doesn't know *anything* about girls. And you sound like my *parents*. I bet your mom doesn't always bug you to be more blond, right?"

"Um, no. That would be . . . strange. And kind of evil."

"Yeah, well, meet my parents, Mr. and Mrs. Evil."

"I was just saying that being a girl must be harder because everybody knows girls don't have as much, you know, not as . . . um . . ."

I was about half a second from getting punched again.

"I was gonna say 'power,'" I said, and Polly raised a fist. "Wait, wait, wait, I'm not done!"

"Now you sound like my *dad*," she said in a growly voice.

"Let me finish! It's lame to say that, right? I'm a boy, but you could probably beat me up with one hand, right?" I tried to be like Max and smile in a really charming way, but it felt totally fake, like I was just opening my mouth and showing my teeth.

Polly glared a second longer, then took a deep breath.

"I totally could," she said.

"I don't care that you're a girl," I said. *Think, Vincent. Think fast.* "I bet Mr. Zazueta didn't either, huh?"

"No," Polly said. She smiled a little—changing the subject actually worked for once! "Well, it's not like he didn't care, but he didn't think it was bad to be a girl. He always said girls are just as powerful as boys, and anyone who didn't think so was full of it."

"Wow, that's really cool!" I said. "Most of the teachers at Kirby suck. They're all, 'let's get you a supply of books that tells the history of stuff nobody cares about, Vincent,' and 'hey, watch this incredibly boring documentary, Vincent.' Like I'd ever watch a documentary that wasn't about Stupendous."

"My dad says stuff like that too," Polly said. "He's all, 'nobody but you can decide what your future will be!'"

"My dad too!" I said. "'Be the hero of your own life!'"

"Yeah." Polly suddenly looked bummed out. "My dad and my mom say stuff like that. Except what they really mean is 'do everything the way I tell you to!'"

"It totally sucks," I said. "My mom's boyfriend is the only grown-up I know who thinks the club's not a total joke."

Which was something I'd never thought about until right that second. Huh.

"I don't think the club's a joke."

Polly looked at me and smiled, and this time it lasted longer than a nanosecond. I smiled back, then dropped my eyes to the ground.

"What I was gonna say about Mr. Zazueta, back at your house . . ." Polly said. "Sometimes I wished *he* was my dad, you know?"

And suddenly I *did* know.

"Yeah. My mom's boyfriend is really cool. Not like my dad at all."

"It's messed up to think about it, though. I feel like a traitor or something."

"Me too."

"I've never said all that stuff to anyone before," Polly said in a low voice.

I scraped up all the tiny specks of courage I had and looked at her. She was still looking at me, and *KAPOW*— it was like an electric shock to make eye contact with her. This time we both looked at the ground.

"Anyway," I said.

"Anyway."

"Pssst, Vincent! Polly!" Max's voice came from back in the trees. "Check this out!"

Polly and I turned away from each other fast—I was relieved by the interruption, but a little bummed out too. We picked our way through the trees, following the random beams of light from Max's and George's flashlights. We found them at the edge of a clearing, maybe a hundred feet back from the edge of the water. It looked like they were drawing a rectangle on the ground with their flashlights.

"Uh, what are you guys doing?" Polly said.

"It's a footprint," Max said, holding his flashlight steady at one point. "See? There's the edge."

"And there's a dead goose." George pointed his flashlight at a spot ten feet in from the edge of the giant footprint.

"Aw, gross." Polly put a hand over her mouth, which made her voice sound kind of muffled. "The poor goose."

I was about to say, *definitely where Mayhem's headquarters is*, but I didn't need to—it became pretty obvious when the clearing was suddenly filled with light, two of the tall trees behind us moved, and we looked up to see the robot, which had been standing there in the dark all along. A big, glowy circle of light blazed from the palms of its hands, which basically blinded us all.

"Stupendify!" Polly changed into Stupendous and launched into the air while Max, George, and I took off running in all directions. I crashed into someone (probably Max) at full speed and we knocked heads, which made a supernova of pain go off inside my skull. To make things even better, I tripped over the edge of the giant robot footprint and went down with a *thud*, landing halfway in and out of the footprint. I heard a *CLANG* from overhead, and Stupendous slammed into the ground right next to me. I rolled away from him purely by instinct, which was good because a second later the robot stomped on him, driving Stupendous even farther into the ground.

Next thing I knew, there was a blast of air and a huge

whooshing noise, then the whole world seemed to explode in dirt, darkness, and metallic *CLANK* sounds. I bounced off the ground, got a big spray of dirt and grass right in the face, and *WHAMMO*, hit the back of my head against something really, really hard. I wondered if Professor Mayhem had decided to kill us all by having his robot jump on top of us like a professional wrestler, but I didn't wonder for very long because I made like a good little robot assault victim and blacked out.

CHAPTER

Waking up hurt. First, I was lying on my back, almost completely buried in dirt and torn-up grass. Second, it felt like all the bones and brains in my head had turned into rotten watermelon. When I touched the back of my skull I was hit by a giant bolt of pain, and I felt something sticky. Bleeding head, oh super. I slowly raised my head, trying not to throw up, and looked down at myself. It looked like a big scoop of the lakeshore had been dumped on the floor, with me mostly under it. My head stuck out of the edge of the pile, and my feet were in the middle of the deepest part. I'd come pretty close to being buried alive. Freaky.

I looked around, trying not to jiggle my bloody skull too much. I was in an enormous room, probably bigger than Corwin Stadium. There was a huge rectangle on the wall to my right, probably a giant-robot-size door.

Stupendous was locked up in some kind of rack—he

dangled from his hands, which were encased in big, cylinder-shaped cuffs of metal. It looked like he was out cold, with his chin on his chest and his eyes closed.

Captain Stupendous has only been knocked unconscious three times—once each by Payload, Harbold the Mighty, and the Cosmonaut. I was not happy to be there for "Unconscious Episode Number Four."

The Stupendous containment gizmo was directly across from me, and the rest of the gigantic room went off to my left. The whole place smelled like a moldy toilet full of wet grass.

The robot stood in front of the giant door. Its eyes flared and went out, and there was a *WHISSSFFFT* sound. The robot's face went *KACHUNK* and swung open, and a thick, flat piece slid out from the robot's head, like a big tongue.

There were rails on either side of the tongue, and Professor Mayhem slid his hands along them as he stepped out. He waved a hand in front of his face and looked up at the ceiling, which had one round skylight. It wasn't much of a skylight—whatever was out there looked dark and green. There were vents all around it.

The front of the tongue slid inward and a thin, metal ladder slid out and went all the way down to the floor. Mayhem tugged on his gloves, turned around, and started climbing down.

Professor Mayhem looked like a shrimpy little guy on TV, but by the time he reached the floor he looked really tall. Also, he must have been in good shape, because that was a long ladder—it took him forever to climb all the way down. I wondered why he didn't put in an elevator or something.

His red lab coat hung open and swished around him like a cape as he pushed the big red goggles up on his old-man forehead and walked over to Stupendous. I played dead, but he didn't even look in my direction. He went right over and jabbed his bony face at Stupendous like it was a face-shaped finger.

Sometime when I wasn't looking Stupendous had

woken up. He glared back at Mayhem. Stupendous jerked his shoulders around a few times but mostly he just gave Mayhem a dirty look.

They stared at each other like that for a while. My leg was pinned in an awkward position and it was getting hard not to twitch when finally Mayhem started talking.

"You're finally awake! Who knew the vaunted Captain

Stupendous was even capable of being unconscious for the lion's share of the day? Why, it makes you seem positively human!"

We'd been out of it for a whole day? Yikes.

Stupendous just stared back at Mayhem with a blank expression. His mouth was a totally straight line—it looked like somebody drew it on his face with a magic marker and a ruler.

"I really thought this would be more fun, Stupendous! Do you mind very much if I call you Stupendous?"

"Fun?" Stupendous said. "This is supposed to be fun?"

"Perhaps 'fun' is the wrong word. I'll be more blunt—I thought it would be more *impressive*."

"To who, crazy man?"

"Haven't you ever tried to impress a young woman, Stupendous?"

"Uh, no."

"Oh, that's right—you're one of those blasted, muscular, lunkhead types who've never HAD to try."

The change in Mayhem's voice and posture was scary—suddenly he sounded like a psycho killer, all snarly and hunched up.

"Uh, hello? No, that's really not it," Stupendous said, but Mayhem was on a roll.

"*Your* ticket in the genetic lottery came through, didn't

it? Never mind that you were probably incapable of any feats of mental dexterity; having oversize biceps was enough, wasn't it? WASN'T IT?"

Mayhem got right up in Stupendous's face and SCREAMED that last part, and Stupendous jerked his head back and to the side.

"You're spitting on me!" he said. "Quit it, loser!"

I took advantage of all the yelling to shift my leg, which was asleep all the way up to my butt. I looked up, and Stupendous was staring at me with a look of surprise, all glowing blue eyes and raised eyebrows. I froze again as Mayhem stepped back from Stupendous. This time he clasped his hands together behind his back and stood with his feet shoulder-width apart.

"'Loser'? I detest that term, Stupendous. How cruel. How very, very cruel."

"*I'm* cruel?"

"Great leaping horned toads, Stupendous, stop repeating every word I say, you sound like a child! Pull yourself together, man!"

"I'm not—"

"Pish, I suppose your actual performance in battle matters less than your overblown reputation. Violet is a perceptive lass—she'll understand the magnitude of my accomplishment."

Mom! Where was she? And was he really trying to *impress her?*

Mayhem gave a piggy snort.

"Why, she has every right to swoon over that full-body shackle that holds you, or my robotic man Friday."

I closed my eyes for just a second and prayed that Stupendous would let Mayhem talk. Sooner or later every supervillain in the universe just has to start bragging about his brilliant plan. I think it's some kind of requirement.

"Isn't your curiosity piqued, old boy?" Mayhem said. "Don't you wish to know how I've so handily defeated you?"

Yes, I thought. *Yes, yes, yes! What's your plan? Where's my mom?*

"No," Stupendous said, and I felt a strong urge to slap myself on the forehead.

"NO?" Mayhem screeched. "NO? The greatest scientific triumph of our time? My crowning achievement? You don't wish to know anything about my masterpiece?"

Mayhem threw his arms in the air.

"In the name of all that's unholy, Stupendous, you're not curious about the substance that portends your defeat? You're not curious about *indestructium?*"

CHAPTER

For once in my life I really, really wished I had something to take notes with.

"My magnum opus, O Captain! my Captain! An impenetrable alloy that can withstand the heat of a star, the pressure of the deepest ocean crevasse, or the cold of interplanetary space! Not even the legendary Captain Stupendous can damage it! Twenty-five years it took me to create it! It's the greatest feat of metallurgy in history!"

Without turning his head, Mayhem pointed at the robot. He really leaned into it, like he was pointing with the whole top half of his body.

"I mastered the intricacies of robotics long ago, of course, but the *alloy*—creating the alloy plagued me for eons. I knew the metals in that meteorite I discovered in high school were out of the ordinary, but it took all of my intellectual skill to fully understand the molecular structure."

!!!

"Ray-Ray Wu had it *easy* in comparison. Creating filaments out of a series of single-molecule chains? Ha! Child's play! Creating the most advanced work of robotics out of an entirely new, indestructible alloy, on the other hand— *that's* real science for you."

He sighed, a big, heavy, fake-sounding sigh.

"That containment device is made of indestructium as well," Mayhem said quietly. "The only way you'll escape it is if you can reduce your body mass by 80 percent. I don't believe that's one of your vaunted abilities."

He tapped his foot a few times.

"I may as well look in on *ma chérie* while I ponder your ultimate fate. I shall return."

Mayhem pivoted and walked off at high speed. I took the risk of lifting my head. Dirt sifted out of my hair as I watched Mayhem stomp off to my left. Our end of the giant room was mostly empty—just the robot door, the actual robot, the Stupendous trap, and my sorry little pile of dirt. There were about twenty rows of big tables starting a couple of hundred feet to my left, and Mayhem muttered and swore as he walked between them. He disappeared from sight, but I heard his footsteps keep going.

After a while they faded out too, and a few seconds after that I heard a distant *WHIZZT* sound.

"He's gone," Stupendous said, staring at the far end of the room. "There are a couple of doors down there, that must be where your mom is. You're really dirty, Vincent."

"Nice. Thanks a lot."

"No, I mean I didn't even see you there—your face is the only part of you that's even showing, and it's got dried mud all over it. It's like you're camouflaged."

"That explains why only one of us is locked up."

"Ha-ha," Stupendous said. "Get up and help me break out of this thing."

"Uh, hello? Professor Mayhem's coming back any second, remember?"

"We have to get out of here!"

"I know, you big dummy! It's MY MOM in there, you know."

"I know that, just—"

There was another distant *WHIZZT* sound, followed by some loud talking from Mayhem. For a second I thought I heard somebody talking back, although I couldn't tell what they were saying.

The talking stopped, and I heard footsteps coming our way. Stupendous darted his eyes away from me and I let my head fall back onto the pile of dirt, thinking it'd be more noticeable if my head was up. I instantly regretted it, of course, and gnashed my teeth together as the pain went through my skull. I managed to keep my eyes open anyway.

Professor Mayhem clip-clopped back across the giant room, his footsteps gradually getting louder and louder. When he walked out from the rows of tables he was holding some kind of long, nasty ray gun in one hand. It was really old-school, like the giant robot—it was made of corroded-looking metal, with a big, round trigger guard. He swung it over his head and back down parallel to the floor. The gun barrel was wrapped with a series of looping rings, and it pointed right at Stupendous's nose.

Stupendous, who'd been trying to squirm around inside the manhole-cover shackle, went totally still and stared at the ray gun. It was close enough to his face to make him go cross-eyed.

"Wha-wha-what is that thing?" he said.

"This?" Mayhem wiggled the tip of the gun. "This is an antimatter pulse rifle, Stupendous."

Huh.

"I don't know if it can actually kill you, given your legendary invulnerability, but I adapted the power cell mechanism from a different shard of that long-ago space projectile. There was a fellow by the name of Miguel

Zazueta who was struck by a different meteorite—I managed to purloin a fragment of it while he lay insensible."

OH NO. It came from the same chunk of space rock that turned Mr. Zazueta into Stupendous? That kind of thing never turns out to be good for the superhero.

"It's remarkably powerful! And if I hold it on you long enough, who knows, you just may expire. Let's test it, shall we?"

"NO!" Stupendous said.

Stupendous thrashed around even more wildly, but the indestructium shackle didn't budge an inch.

"No, wait! What about Vincent's mom?"

Mayhem lifted an eyebrow.

"Who?"

Stupendous stared into the barrel of the gun. His eyes were almost all blue glow and no actual eye. He gulped.

"If you kill me, I'm SO going to beat your face in," he said, but his voice quivered.

"Oh, I'm not going to kill you, Stupendous. Not yet. I'm just going to find out if I CAN kill you. Hold still, please."

He pulled the trigger, and a beam of strange light rocketed out of the gun and hit Stupendous right in the face. The light was blue, but it was the weirdest shade of blue ever—it was dark blue. I didn't think a beam of light could be dark, but it was. Stupendous screamed so loudly that my ears hurt, and his body arched way out, arms and legs fully extended.

For a split second the world went fuzzy and everything started to look farther away than it really was—it was too much. My brain was collapsing in on itself. But Captain Stupendous was SCREAMING! Would this kill him? What would happen when Stupendous died? Would he turn back into Polly? Would Polly be lying there dead on the floor? Polly!

"STOP!" I shouted.

Mayhem whipped his head in my direction and looked at me over his shoulder, one eyebrow arched way up on his wrinkled, old man's forehead. He shut off the death beam and pointed the gun back at the ceiling. Stupendous went limp and dangled by his shoulders.

Mayhem walked over to me, stopped between me and Stupendous, and pointed the ray gun at me. I tried to leap to my feet all at once, but that's hard to do when you're mostly buried. I jerked partly up, fell back, and caught myself with my elbows and crab-crawled with my arms and legs until I could stand.

My head was still pounding, but I was amped. The threat of death by antimatter rifle made the blood rush through my whole body.

"Good lord, it's a stringy cockroach of a boy," Mayhem
said. "How did you get into my stronghold, boy?"

I'd never been called "boy" before—I guess I don't have
enough pompous old men in my life—and I didn't like it
much. "Stringy cockroach" wasn't too great either.

I was so, so sick of people talking smack to me.

"You brought me in here, dingleberry, figure it out."

Mayhem shook his head and lowered his ray gun. I started shaking all over—you just don't realize how cool it is to have no guns pointed at you until somebody stops pointing one at you. Then Mayhem laughed, one short, hard woof of laughter.

"Who are you, boy?"

I almost blurted out, *Vincent Wu*! That would have been stupid, though, and even in the middle of all the craziness I managed to remember something Stupendous said in *Stupendous on Stupendous*: Civilians should never identify themselves to the enemy.

"Nobody," I said. "Just a fan of Captain Stupendous."

"Are you, now?" Mayhem had this look on his face, like he'd just heard the funniest thing ever. "A fan of Captain Stupendous! How wonderful! Do you fancy yourself a hero as well, boy? Are you going to thrash me and save the day?"

I snuck a peek over Mayhem's shoulder at Stupendous, but he wasn't paying attention at all—his face was all the way down on his chest, his eyes were nonglowing and blank, and his shoulders were slumped.

Captain Stupendous was out of it, and who knew where Max and George were? I was alone with a supervillain. But that was what I always wanted, right? Just like Mayhem said . . . my chance to save the day. Except I was probably gonna die instead. In front of my hero, who turns out to be a girl, and not just any girl, but Polly Winnicott-Lee! All of a sudden I wanted to beat somebody's brains in.

"I'm gonna beat your brains in," I said.

"Beg pardon?"

"You heard me, whack job! Come on, fight like a man!"

I put my fists up, and it must have been obvious I had no idea how to fight because Mayhem burst out laughing again.

"Boy, you must be joking! Look at you, you wouldn't last thirty seconds! A girl could knock you senseless!"

Stupendous raised his head. His eyes started glowing again, and he clamped his mouth shut in a hard, straight line.

"Why are supervillains so full of themselves?" I said. "You're all the same, every one of you!"

Mayhem tensed up and stood straighter with a little jerk.

"I'll thank you to keep a civil tongue in your head, boy," he said.

"You ARE all the same!" I shouted. "You just talk and talk, blah-blah-blah, 'I'm so great, I'm so smart, I'm so much better than you.' You're such total BULLIES. But you all end up making some incredibly dumb mistake, every time. You're all losers!"

Mayhem stiffened. He stood up really straight and looked down his nose at me. I could actually see his nostril hairs from that angle.

"Hold your tongue, you little swine," he said.

"Loser," I said, still holding up my fists. "You're gonna lose, and you know it, because you're a loser. Luh-luh-luh-LOOOOOOOOOSER!"

"Your hero is about to enter oblivion, you foulmouthed, little wretch. But fear not, you may accompany him. Ta."

Mayhem pointed the gun at me again, but I saw something that freaked me out in a totally different way. Over Mayhem's shoulder there was a flash of blue light.

Captain Stupendous changed back into Polly.

CHAPTER

There was a muffled thud—probably Polly hitting the floor, since the full-body shackle was way too big to hold her—and Mayhem flicked his head to the side for just a second.

I let out a demented-rooster war cry, jumped forward, and grabbed the gun with both hands. By some miracle I got hold of the gun's barrel and stuffed it under my arm so I wouldn't get shot in the face. Mayhem staggered backward and I lost my balance, dragging his arm down to the floor. I tried to tie my arms into a knot around the gun, and when Mayhem reached for me with his free hand, I snapped my teeth at it.

"Ye gods, boy, are you some type of savage?"

Mayhem snarled and pulled his hand back, then lifted his gun hand, with me wrapped around it, until I was standing again. Mayhem was strong! Who knew? He made a fist and, *PAPOW*, hit me right in the face.

Sadly, this was not the first time I'd been punched in the face—Scott Fanelli cornered me in a stairwell last year and socked me in the eye for using words with more than two syllables—but Mayhem was even worse than a middle-school bully. I howled as Mayhem grabbed the front of my shirt and hauled me off my feet. He shook me like I was a cheap plastic utility belt and hissed into my face—no words, just hissing.

"Wow, you are a freak," I said.

Then my head remembered how bashed-in it was, my stomach realized how much toxic swill was sloshing around in it, and I threw up. A bellyful of puke hit Professor Mayhem right smack in his ugly, evil face.

He said something like "AAARRRHHFFFVVGGGHH!" and tried to throw me, but I still had his gun hand in a hammerlock, and my weight pulled him down sideways. I landed on my feet but I had nothing left in the tank, so I lost my grip and fell to the floor. Mayhem jerked away and slapped his hands over his eyes. He spun halfway around just as Polly stepped out from behind him and swiped the gun away with her foot. Mayhem stood up straight, trying to wipe the barf out of his eyes, and Polly did a karate spin move and kicked him in the solar plexus.

I was pretty sure that's where she kicked him, anyway, because Mayhem doubled over and started gasping like a dying goldfish. He bobbed his head up and down, wrapped his arms around his stomach, stepped in a greasy puddle of vomit, did a cartoony, running-in-place thing for two steps, and toppled over backward. The back of his head hit the floor, *KACHUNK*, and he slumped flat on his back, eyes closed and hands flopped out to either side.

I propped myself up on one elbow. Polly kept her eyes on Mayhem as she walked over and kneeled on the floor next to me. I used the crook of my other elbow to wipe a little bit of vomit off the corner of my mouth. Then I looked cross-eyed at my nose.

"Is it broken?" I poked at it with one finger.

"I don't think so," Polly said. "That was, like, the mother of all pukes."

"Geez, kick a guy while he's down. . . ."

"No, you took him out by barfing on him. It's good. Disgusting, but good."

My head still hurt, but the good thing about throwing up is at least it makes you stop wanting to throw up. I stood up, feeling like a hundred-year-old man, but I forgot about that when Polly started shaking.

Her hands shook first, and the shaking ran up her arms and down the whole length of her body. She took a step forward and kind of fell into me, and I barely managed to catch her without falling over myself. She made a thick noise, like crying and swallowing at the same time, then breathed in and out really fast as I stood there with my arms around her.

Now that was complicated, because Polly was seriously losing her marbles, and all I could think about was what it felt like to hug a real live girl. I patted her on the shoulder with one hand while I tried to figure out what to do with my other hand. Eventually I just left it hanging in midair.

After a couple of minutes—actually I had no idea how long it was, it could have been an hour—she elbowed my arms off her and took a step back, pressing the heels of her palms to her eyes.

"Sorry," she said.

"It's okay." I wasn't sure what she was sorry about—getting tortured by Professor Mayhem would make anyone freak out.

We looked at Mayhem again, keeping a few feet away from him. When you're dealing with the worst villain in history, it pays to be a little cautious.

"Oh gross, his head's all bloody," I said.

"Good," Polly said in a growly voice. She grabbed her elbows with her hands and shivered. "If I had an electric guitar, I'd smash it against his ugly face."

"You think he's dead?" I said.

"Does it look like I care?"

"Yeah, but still . . . I've never killed anybody."

"Me either, but we don't need to worry about it—he's still breathing." She pointed at Mayhem's chest, which was going slowly up and down. "Let's find your mom and get out of here," Polly said.

We looked toward the other end of the room—if you rolled a basketball across the floor, it probably would have vanished into the distance. When we were looking that way the Stupendous trap was to our right, the robot and its giant robot door were behind us, and a bank of big, flat-screen video monitors was to our left. The rows of tables stretched out in front of us, looking like they went on forever. The tables were covered with mad scientist projects, and each one was probably as big as the whole fan club headquarters.

We walked over to the video screens. Most of them showed places around the city—the torn-up mess at Corwin Stadium, Corwin Plaza, Copperplate Bay, city hall. One screen was all murky green, with a vague, dark shape that might have been a dome at the bottom.

"That's where we are, huh? The bottom of the lake?" Polly said.

"Yeah."

"So we're underwater. Great. How are we gonna get out of here without drowning?"

"You're not gonna drown. Captain Stupendous doesn't need to breathe, I'm the one who's gonna have problems."

"Well, geez, Vincent, that's no good either," Polly said. She put her hand on my arm, right above the elbow.

Despite the aftertaste of barf in my mouth and the three or four hundred bruises all over me, what I felt right then was a warm, fizzy vibration where Polly's hand touched my arm.

I'm not saying I was happy about it, just so you know. I'm just saying I was aware of it.

"Hey, uh, thanks," she said. "For, you know, saving my life."

Oh great, time for some mushy talk. Yeah, my heart was thumping kind of fast, and my palms itched, but it wasn't because of the drippy thank-you stuff, or Polly touching me on the arm or anything.

"That's cool," I said.

Polly arched one eyebrow. She let go of me, crossed her arms, and stared at me with a smile that was . . . well, I couldn't tell what kind of smile it was. Only one side of her mouth went up, and she shook her head back and forth reeeeeeally slowly.

"What?" I said.

Polly smiled with both sides of her mouth, went *hmmmfff* through her nose, then combed her hair backward with one hand. A few sweaty-looking strands stuck out from the sides of her head and floated over her ears. Out of nowhere I found myself wanting her to smile really widely, just so I could see the gap between her front teeth.

"Nothing, Vincent. You're just such a . . . such a *boy*."

Girls are so bizarre! It's like they don't know how to talk like regular people.

"I don't see your mom up there," Polly said, scanning the rest of the screens.

"Me neither, but I think I heard her talking to Mayhem before."

"Right, by those doors over there!" Polly pointed at the far end of the room. "There must be a jail cell or something."

We started walking to the other end of the big room, looking for doors. I pointed at a bright red car covered with long, curved spikes, with wires and tools and shiny metal parts piled up around it.

"Check it out, porcupine car."

"Boy, he really likes the color red," Polly said, laying a hand on the porcupine car's fender.

"I guess," I said. "We need something airtight to get out with. A porcupine car would be airtight, wouldn't it?"

Polly rubbed her forehead with one palm.

"I don't see a key," she said. "I guess I could break the windows, but . . ."

"That'd make the whole thing kind of pointless," I said. We kept looking.

There was SO much freaky stuff just lying around. There was a huge, wired-together skeleton with twenty legs standing on one table, like something from a museum of natural history for monsters. Another table was covered by big metal boxes with funky writing carved into their sides. One table had nothing but a giant robot torso on it, with the chest opened up. There was a spare foot on a different table, and a spare head on another, with the face slid open like the door of a minivan. The spare parts were brighter and shinier than the robot, which was darker gray, and had a rougher texture.

"I don't think these are made out of indestructium," I said. "Just regular metal."

With all the crazy villain devices lying around, it was weird to see things like pencils and rolls of duct tape, but there was a pile of that stuff on one of the tables too. A spiral notebook lay open on the table with the spare head. There was a sketch of the robot on the open page, with the arms spinning around. Mayhem had drawn a few curved lines to make it look like the arms were going really fast. Something caught my eye, mostly because it looked familiar—it was in the corner of a clear plastic box, partly hidden behind a few random chunks of polished metal. It was a gyroscope.

"Hey, I have one of these," I said, holding it up for Polly to see. She shrugged.

"Great," she said. "You guys have the same taste in toys. Let's get going, Vincent."

"Yeah, yeah," I said. I slid the notebook along the edge of the table in Polly's direction. "Look at this, though. I think he modeled the robot's spinning arm thing after this gyroscope."

"Congratulations on finding a souvenir."

I stuck the gyroscope in my pocket as we kept walking. We passed the last table and walked into an empty space the same size as the one at the other end of the giant room, only with no robot or body shackles. There were two doors in the far wall—at least they looked like doors. They were really just two big slabs of metal in the wall. Each one had a glowing panel of either metal or plastic in the wall next to it at about neck height for me, although they were probably elbow-high for Mayhem. I put my hand on one—it glowed more brightly for a second, but nothing happened.

"She's gotta be in one of those rooms," Polly said.

"Yeah. Can you change into Stupendous and break them down?"

Polly groaned, and her shoulders drooped. "Sure. Stupendify!"

Captain Stupendous instantly appeared in Polly's place, with his shoulders in the exact same droopy position.

"The only time anyone tries to kill me—literally kill me—is when I'm in this body," she said.

"You would have had to change into this form anyway," I said. "You can't show your secret identity to my mom."

"Yeah, yeah."

Stupendous rubbed his face, then raised a fist up to head level.

"Don't bash it in all the way, you might squish her."

"I'm not a moron, Vincent."

Stupendous pounded once on the door, almost like he was knocking. It wasn't much more than a tap on the Stupendous scale, but the door partially crumpled anyway.

"Dennis?" a voice said, from inside the room. It was Mom, and I felt relief go through me—it was an actual physical feeling, like having a bucket of water poured over your head. Mom was alive.

"GET AWAY FROM THE DOOR," Stupendous hollered.

"Okay," Mom said a couple of seconds later, in a fainter voice.

Stupendous pounded on the door again. He hit it a lot

harder, though, and the door screeched and collapsed into the room, landing on the floor with a *CLANG*.

Stupendous and I stepped into a room about the size of my homeroom at school. On our left there was a chair and a table covered with stacks of books and papers, and on our right was a twin-size bed pushed up against the wall, with Mom sitting on it. She stood up, and when she spoke she sounded about as confused as I've ever heard her.

"Vincent! And Captain Stupendous?" she said. Before I could stop myself I ran over and hugged her, and she hugged me back hard. It should have felt embarrassing and annoying to do that in front of Stupendous, but it didn't. Mom leaned back and put her hands on my cheeks, which *was* embarrassing and annoying for her to do in front of Stupendous. I twisted my head out of her grip.

"Geez, Mom, don't do that."

"What are you doing here?"

What kind of stupid question was that?

"I got caught in the middle of a fight," I said.

"Are you, um, okay . . . ma'am?" Stupendous asked.

"I'm fine, I'm fine. Dennis is psychologically unstable but I don't believe he'd actually hurt me," Mom said, brushing off her skirt. She tilted her head to look at Stupendous. "What possessed you to bring my son down here, Captain?"

Oh, for crying out loud . . .

Stupendous shifted from one foot to the other.

"I don't know," he said.

"Mom, did you and Dad really go to high school with Professor Mayhem?"

"Yes, Vincent, and I'll tell you all the details, I promise. But we should get to safety first, don't you think?"

"Um, yeah, let's get out of here," I said. "I think—"

"Did you hear something?" Stupendous said. He spun around and walked out of the room. Mom and I hustled after him.

We were halfway across the giant room, so the robot was pretty far away. We were still close enough to see a tiny person reach the top of the ladder and stagger into the robot's head, though. The tongue walkway pulled back into the head, the robot's face slid down into place, and the glassy robot eyes lit up.

"Oh, you've gotta be kidding," I said.

CHAPTER

"Why didn't we tie him up?" Stupendous held his hands in front of his face, like claws, then clenched them into fists and lowered them down to chest level. He stepped backward with one foot, looking ready to fly, but Mom grabbed his arm.

"Wait," she said. "Look at him."

The robot took a couple of lurching steps forward, looking like it might lose its balance.

"He doesn't look so good," I said.

"Duh," Stupendous said. "He was bleeding all over the place, you know."

"What happened?" Mom's head swiveled back and forth between me and Stupendous.

"Um, Captain Stupendous knocked out Professor Mayhem," I said, trying to think fast. "Mayhem hit his head on the floor."

"He must have a concussion," Mom said. "And a cut on his scalp—head wounds bleed a lot."

"Good," Stupendous said. "Makes it easy to take him down."

Mom smiled at Stupendous in a tight-lipped way. "Dennis is a fighter, Captain. He always has been, even if he hasn't always looked the part."

"Also, he's still inside an indestructible giant robot," I said. "That kind of makes up for the concussion."

It took the robot three steps to reach the spot where the tables full of mad scientist junk started, and it stopped there, looking down. For a crazy second I wondered if he was looking for his missing gyroscope. Gyroscope . . . gyroscope . . .

DING, DING, DING! I dug into my pocket in a panic, and as I pulled out Mayhem's gyroscope I thought of the clearest plan I'd ever thought of, all the way from start to finish, like a movie inside my brain. *The gyroscope was the key to defeating Professor Mayhem!*

I looked around frantically and saw the spare robot head. *BING!* That was our way out. "The spare head!"

"What about the spare head?" Stupendous said, keeping his eyes on the robot.

"You can give us a ride out of here inside it," I said.

Mom looked over at the head. "It's a shame it's not made of indestructium," she said.

"You know about indestructium too?" Stupendous said.

"I've been here for a while, remember. And Dennis has always loved the sound of his own voice."

Mayhem's robot took one step between the tables and stopped, like Mayhem didn't want to bust up his own stuff.

"Once we're outside, we launch Plan B," I said, hoping Stupendous would just go along with it.

"Plan B? You wanna refresh my memory?"

Sheesh. Max and George would have taken the hint the first time.

"Plan B! *Remember?*"

Professor Mayhem, of all people, saved me from having to bluff it out any longer. "CURSES!" he yelled, and totally stomped one of his own mad scientist tables into bits as he came after us.

"Now!" I said. "Bash a hole in the ceiling and get us out of here—go!"

Stupendous launched straight up while Mom and I sprinted for the table with the spare head. There was a *CRASH* overhead, and as I climbed onto the table I felt a few drops of water sprinkle down on me. There was a *THUMP* on the floor behind me, then another *CRASH* from the ceiling. I climbed up into the spare head and pawed all around the inside, looking for some way to close up the face as Mom climbed in after me.

"NO!" Mayhem's voice yelled. "WHERE ARE YOU GOING, VIOLET? STAY WITH ME!" I heard a glassy *CRUNCH*, a metallic *RRRRIPPP*, and the *CLANG* of giant robot footsteps.

I also heard one more *CRASH* from the ceiling, and I saw a stinky, green waterfall appear over Mom's shoulder. Then Stupendous's upside-down head appeared, looking into the spare head from above.

"Get inside!" he said. There was a big, padded chair in the middle of the head, with a big egg-shaped helmet on the seat.

"You take the seat, Vincent," Mom said.

Fine by me! I tossed the helmet to the side and sat in the chair. Stupendous's head disappeared, and the face suddenly clamped shut, *BANG*. Of course, it was totally dark inside the spare head. I had the feeling that putting on a seat belt wasn't a bad idea, so I felt all around the seat for straps and buckles. Nothing. A spare head that Mayhem wasn't finished making—well, that was just super.

KACHUGGANUNK!

KAWHUMP!

KAWHAAAAMMMMM!

It sounded like Stupendous and the robot were really cracking skulls out there. The spare head jerked around like crazy. I grabbed at the sides of the chair, but I missed my grip and toppled out. If I had a dollar for every time I'd fallen over since meeting Polly Winnicott-Lee, I could have bought a new porcupine car.

Mom kept her balance at first, but she tried to grab me as I fell out of the chair, which made her lose her grip on the chair and fall over too.

"Mom!"

"I'm oka—OW! I mean, I'm okay!"

The spare head was suddenly filled with creaking, squealing sounds, like metal being scraped against metal. Then the whole thing lurched up like a nightmare elevator. I fell forward, smacked into the wall with both hands and the side of my face, tumbled sideways, and collided with Mom. She went "OOF" when my head hit her in the side. Finally I got hung up in a mess of wires, my head spinning, as the feeling of going up started again. When my head cleared I felt water soaking through the back of my clothes.

How deep was Lake Higgleman? It couldn't be that deep, right? I grabbed a bunch of the wires and dragged myself more or less upright, so at least I wouldn't drown.

"Vincent, keep your head above water!" Mom screamed. *No kidding, Mom.*

We must have reached the surface, because I heard a *PFOOMPF* as we tilted and speeded up. I fell and landed butt first, and momentum pinned me against the wall as lake water flooded my pants.

THUNK! It felt like we'd reached dry ground! Hallelujah! Stupendous tore the face right off of the robot's head, and water spilled out onto the greenish mud of the lakeshore. I saw the sky—oh, it was awesome to see the sky—and Stupendous was shouting.

"OVER HERE! OVER HERE!"

"Over where?" I yelled. "What are you—"

But Stupendous blasted off without answering. The spare robot head was looking mostly up, so I couldn't see

the surface of the lake, but the robot appeared like an evil sun coming up over the horizon. Stupendous flew out to meet it, with his cape swooping out behind him.

"COME BACK, YOU COWARD!" Mayhem's voice said.

"YOU GOT IT!" Stupendous said.

Mom and I flailed our way out of the tangled-up wires. I used the chair to climb out of the spare head, while Mom just hoisted herself up over the edge and hopped down into the mud, looking pretty smooth while she did it. I stared at her as she straightened out her skirt.

"Nice jump, Mom."

"Don't sound so surprised! I played volleyball in college, you know."

Mom glanced over my shoulder and her eyes opened up really wide. "HEY! OVER HERE!"

I turned around to see who Mom was yelling "over here" to. Running toward the robot head were Max, George, and . . . Bobby?

Yep, it was Detective Boyfriend Bobby Carpenter. Behind them, parked right in front of the trees, was a police helicopter. What? Why? Huh? It was light out, but the sun was definitely on its way down. We'd been locked up in Mayhem's headquarters for a whole freaking day.

"Vincent!" George yelled as the three of them slipped and slid up to us.

"What's up, dude?" Max said. He punched me in the arm. I was so amped up that I barely felt it. Then George punched me on the arm too, which I did feel, if only from surprise. George never hits anybody.

"I told you!" he said to Max. "I told you Vincent would make it out of there!"

"You were right, little dude," Max said, giving George a fist bump.

"Don't call me little dude, dude."

It was cool that George and Max were so happy about me not being dead, but I was also a little distracted by the sight of Bobby going to Mom without a word and hugging her really, really tightly. She hugged him back and pressed her face into his shoulder, and it was a quick hug, but still SO, SO embarrassing. They let go of each other, and Bobby turned to look at me and the guys.

"What do you know," Bobby said, with a grin. "You boys were absolutely right."

I looked at Bobby, and he grabbed my shoulders with both hands and gave me a little shake.

"Vincent, you amaze me," Bobby said, and how many people ever said that to me before then? That's right, exactly zero. I didn't want a goofy smile to take over my whole face, but I couldn't help it.

"You're alive!" George said. "And you're inside a giant robot head, that's so cool!"

"George was really worried," Max said, leaning in close to me and cupping the side of his mouth with one hand.

"Oh, and what, you were cool as a cucumber? Vincent, Max totally cried when Mayhem grabbed you!"

"Oh, that's it, I'm gonna kill you, little dude."

"Boys, please. Are you hurt, Vincent?" Bobby said with a frown. He reached out a hand and gently turned my face to one side.

"I'm fine," I said, leaning back just far enough to pull away from his hand. "Just a couple of bruises. Professor Mayhem's the one who's in really bad shape." I pointed at the sky.

Captain Stupendous was fighting, and not just flailing away like he was in the first three robot battles—he was going off. The Corkscrew, the Double Helix, the Double-clutch Piston Kick, he was throwing everything in the book out there. Mayhem was definitely hurting, because the robot was a little slower and less coordinated than before. Stupendous was landing every single one of his punches.

And none of it mattered, because the robot didn't even have a tiny, little dent on it. Stupid indestructible metal.

"So it's true," Mom said. "He really did create an impervious alloy."

"Imperviwhat?" Max said in a low voice. George leaned over to listen while I filled Max in.

"Violet, we have to get these boys to safety," Bobby said in a total I'm-taking-command-of-the-situation voice.

"I agree, Detective," Mom said. It was a relief to see them shift out of hugging mode.

"NO," I said. "Not yet." I yanked Mayhem's gyroscope out of my pocket and held it up.

"Hey, I have an idea," Max said. "We should—"

"You know what, I wanna—" George was talking more to Max than anybody else.

"Boys, now isn't—" Mom said.

"Vincent, is this the time for—" Bobby said.

Everyone was talking at the same time, and I was so over it. Mom was standing on the beach instead of inside Mayhem's HQ because of *me*. Okay, because of Stupendous too, but he couldn't have done it without *me*. It was time for everybody to listen to *me*!

"LISTEN UP!" I hollered. Max let his mouth hang open for a second, then clamped it shut.

"The robot's designed like one of these. I saw the draw-
ings in Mayhem's headquarters." I barked it out like a sadistic
drill sergeant in a war movie, held up Mayhem's gyroscope,
and spun the centerpiece with my finger. "That's how we can
beat it, by tangling it with a string like I always do with *my*
gyroscope!"

CLANG! Stupendous went whizzing by overhead. He
did a cartwheel in the air, reversed direction, and flew
back into battle.

"Are we thinking the same thing, Vincent?" Mom said, taking me by surprise. "Your father's work, right?"

My eyes must have bulged out of my head or something, because she chuckled.

"I still know your father pretty well. You're thinking about a special kind of filament."

"Yeah. A carbon nanotube monofilament."

You could almost see the lightbulb appear over Max's and George's heads.

"Mad scientist versus regular scientist, winner take all," Max said. "Awesome."

Bobby had an intense, crinkled-eyebrow expression, and I realized how smart it was for Max and George to bring him along. I have the most awesome friends ever.

"How are you going to get the monofilament to Captain Stupendous, Vincent?" Bobby said. "And will he know what to do with it?"

"Yeah, yeah, we have a backup plan," I said. "But we have to get to Corwin Towers right away, can you take us?"

And what do you know, Bobby came through with exactly the right answer. After a second he gave me a fast, crisp nod.

"Let's go."

The helicopter pilot didn't say a word when the five of

us climbed in. He just nodded when Bobby gave the order to take off, and up we went.

"This is the Corwin ViperStrike," Mom said as she buckled up. "Janet really went all out."

Mom, coming through with the knowledge about military aircraft! I was starting to wonder if I knew her at all.

"Ms. Corwin spared no expense to ensure your safety, Violet," Bobby said.

Wanna know what a crazy week it'd been? I was actually a little bored taking off in a police helicopter, although I had to admit it was more comfortable than flying with Stupendous. At least I was inside the helicopter instead of flapping around in the breeze. Also, I was with George and Max and my mom this time.

"How did you guys get Bobby to come to the lake?" I said.

Max held something out in one hand. It was Bobby's card, with a little mud smeared on it.

"You dropped that during the robot's sneak attack," Max said.

"It's kind of a miracle that we found it," George said.

"Bobby waited with us at the lake for a long time," Max said. "George wouldn't let him leave."

George shrugged. "I told him about all the times law

enforcement officers actually helped save superheroes, and he told us about Hummingbird, and I don't know, we just kept talking."

"Did you really cry?" I asked Max.

"Uh, yeah, let's not talk about that."

"Okay, Vincent," Bobby said, looking at me over his shoulder. "What's your plan for delivering the filame—"

"Carpenter," Tom the Pilot said. He tapped a screen in front of him. "Behind us."

Bobby was in the seat next to the pilot, Mom was next to Bobby, and George, Max, and I were in the seats behind them. Max was right behind Bobby, and George and I craned our necks to look out the window on Max's side of the helicopter.

"Oh man, gimme a break," I said.

It figured. The robot was following us.

CHAPTER

"GO, TOM!" Bobby shouted.

Tom the Silent Helicopter Pilot nodded, and we banked hard to the side, straightened out, and headed toward downtown. I caught a glimpse of Mayhem's robot with its hands reaching out. Then it was behind us, which made me even more nervous.

Bobby punched a few buttons on the helicopter radio.

"Corwin Towers security, this is Detective Carpenter of the Copperplate City Police Force!" he barked. "I have the superintendent of schools!"

"Copy, Detective," a bored-sounding voice said after a quick burst of static. "You're cleared for landing."

"Evasive maneuvers!" Silent Tom yelled. He sent the helicopter into some kind of insane tilt-a-whirl move. The guys and I all screamed hysterically as our seat belts locked in place. A giant robot hand appeared outside my window for a second, then jerked out of sight.

"Stupendous has engaged the robot," Tom the Suddenly Talkative Pilot said. "We're in the clear."

"I told you!" Bobby said. He grinned at us.

The towers came into view, casting huge shadows across the length of Corwin Plaza. The two buildings were connected by a fancy-pants glass-and-metal bridge. One roof was covered with plants and grass, like it was a fake park, with benches and streetlights and even a pond. The other rooftop was mostly empty. There was a railing and a set of steps going down into the roof at each corner, a bunch of giant metal tubes for air-conditioning, or whatever those giant tubes are used for. Most of the rooftop was taken up by a big square of empty cement with a circle painted in its center.

We landed, and Bobby popped the door open while the chopper was still running. A bunch of serious-looking guys in dark suits ran up the steps, coming at us from all four corners of the building. They all had the same buzz cuts and superstraight posture.

"Detective, Superintendent," one of them said. He nodded to Bobby and Mom as the other men in black herded us all toward a corner of the building. "This way."

We hustled down one of the staircases, through a thick

steel door at the bottom of the stairs, and into an elevator that probably could have held a fire truck. I could barely hold still as we went down. Were we taking too long? Was Stupendous holding on?

We raced down a hallway and into an office the size of an airport. There was a bunch of tables and couches and stuff on the end of the room closest to the door, then nothing but carpet for about a mile and a half. The far wall was just a giant window with another desk in front of it. An old lady with white hair sat behind the desk, checking her cell phone—in fact, it was the same old lady who'd hung out with me and Dad when the cops first took me in. Janet somebody. She was practically dead, she was so old.

"Violet!" she said. I was surprised by how loud her voice was. She came around the desk, grabbed both of Mom's hands, and held them tight.

"Hello, Janet." Mom had a big smile on her face. "Thanks for going to so much trouble."

"Oh fiddle-faddle," the old lady said. "It was a special occasion."

"Captain Stupendous needs our help," Mom said.

"Does he now?"

"We need to bring him some of your carbon nanotube monofilaments," I said.

Janet (probably Corwin, I suddenly realized) raised her eyebrows at me.

"Err, excuse me," I said. "Can we? Please?"

"Such a well-mannered young man," she said. "Of course, young man, I'll do everything in my power to help Captain Stupendous."

Wow, just like that. I really wasn't used to adults saying yes that easily.

"Really?" I said.

"Really," she said. "You don't know who I am, do you?"

"Uh . . . you're the owner of the company."

"Oh, I'm more than that." She smiled. "I'm also a founding member of the Friends of Stupendous."

The Friends of Stupendous? Those shriveled-up old ladies with their walkers and tiny dogs? I must have drooled or something, because Janet Corwin threw her head back and laughed.

"Captain Stupendous has saved this company from villains more times than I can count, young man. I owe him everything."

George, Max, and I grinned at each other, and for a change the guys weren't doing their annoying fake sibling rivalry thing. Max raised a fist, probably to punch me on the shoulder, but our phones all started ringing again. Janet Corwin already had her phone in her hand.

"Professor Mayhem is here," she said. I looked at my phone.

STUPENDOUS ALERT: GIANT ROBOT. CORWIN TOWERS.

There was a huge *BOOM* from somewhere outside, and the floor shook.

"Safety measures, Mendoza," Janet said. "Call down to R&D and have a spool of filament brought up to the landing pad entrance."

Security Guy Mendoza nodded and ran out of the office, while barking into a walkie-talkie.

"Bobby, let's go," I said, yanking on Bobby's sleeve.

"Vincent, you're staying here," Mom said.

"Forget it, I'm going!" I said.

"So are we!" George said. Max nodded his head.

"VINCENT—"

"Your mother's right, Vincent," Bobby said.

"No, she's not!" I said, spinning around to face Bobby.

"Vincent, you've done extraordinary things," Bobby said. "You helped Captain Stupendous rescue your mom from Professor Mayhem! I'll take it from here. Just tell me what Stupendous expects me to do."

"He's expecting ME," I said. "It won't work if I'm not there!"

I was bluffing, of course—Stupendous wasn't expecting a thing—but there was no way Bobby would go along with my real plan. It was too insane.

"Bobby, you know about helicopters and villains in this town," George said. "Remember Blitzkrieg?"

"If Stupendous sees a helicopter without Vincent inside, he won't know it's there to deliver the monofilament," Max said, and seriously, does anybody have more amazing friends than I do?

"Vincent, I am NOT letting this happen," Mom said.

"There's no choice." I folded my arms, planted my feet, and stared at Bobby. Bobby stared back, frowning. I had to fold my arms, because if I didn't, Bobby would see my hands shaking. Standing up to a bunch of adults who practically run the world is freaky, you know?

Bobby looked at Janet Corwin.

"Ms. Corwin, Vincent's father is in the building, can you get him up here?"

Janet Corwin smiled and shook her head.

"Raymond's sector of the building is in full security lockdown," she said.

"Why aren't you in full security lockdown too?" I said.

"What, and miss getting a bird's-eye view of the action? When this is all over I'll tell you about the summer I lived in Boomtown, when Blue Blazes defeated the Luddite. I was thirteen."

Suddenly I wanted to be friends with Janet Corwin.

Bobby shook his head.

"You win, Vincent, let's go," he said.

"WHAT?" Mom had her fists clenched, which was an unusual look for her.

"There's no time to argue, Violet. But you two stay here!" He said that last part to Max and George.

"NO WAY!" Max said. "We're sticking together!"

"Yeah, we're a TEAM," George said.

"I know," Bobby said. "But I can't justify taking all three of you up there. Let's go, Vincent."

I almost tried one last time to change his mind about Max and George, but, dude, we were out of time.

"Sorry, guys," I said as Bobby and I took off running.

"Both our necks are on the line, Vincent," Bobby said as we reached the elevators. A bunch of new security guys went running past as we got in the elevator. "You're sure Stupendous is expecting this?"

Well, no.

"Yeah," I said. "We planned it all out during our escape. We have to . . . make it look like the helicopter's spinning out of control, and when Stupendous sees me inside it we'll make the exchange."

"We'll have problems if he doesn't see you," Bobby said.

"He has superpowered vision, he can see tiny, little things from a mile away. Literally."

I still needed to tell Stupendous what to do with Dad's Amazing Wonder String, though, just to make sure. History is full of superheroes and bad guys who get beat because they had the key to victory in their hands without knowing it.

We got out of the elevator and ran back to the steel door that led up to the roof. A couple of security guys were there, along with a girl who looked like a teenager, with her big, chunky glasses and her brown hair in a ponytail. She wore a white lab coat, though, so she must have been a scientist. She held out a cylinder of metal the size of a soda bottle, and Bobby grabbed it without even breaking stride.

Up on the roof, Tom the Pilot had the engine running, and my hair was blown every which way as Bobby and I ran to the helicopter and climbed in. Bobby used one hand to pull the door down into place with a *THUNK*. There was a window in the door, big enough for both rows of passengers to see out—I tapped on it with my knuckles.

"Does this open?" I asked Tom the Pilot.

"Affirmative," he said as we roared up off the helicopter pad. He fiddled with his armrest, and a rectangular panel slid open on my armrest, revealing a toggle switch. "Push that switch forward, the window slides open horizontally."

I eyeballed the window. It looked just big enough for my real plan.

We took off, and I looked out over Corwin Plaza as the roof dropped out from under us.

"Up! Go up!" I said. "We have to get over them!"

"Do it, Tom," Bobby said.

Silent Tom shook his head like he thought it was a bad idea, but we were thrown back in our seats as the chopper lurched and buzzed up at an angle. It would be bad if Stupendous did a Meteor Strike just as the helicopter flew over him, but I remembered what he said on that downtown rooftop after that first battle at the school district offices.

I hate those helicopters! Let them out of your sight for one second and they fly right in front of you!

He'd see the chopper. I was betting everything on it.

The sun was going down, and the trees and shops around the edge of Corwin Plaza had long shadows stretching out behind them. The robot was halfway in the shade of Corwin Towers, but its other half reflected the sunlight in all directions. The fountain in the middle of the plaza was smashed under the robot's feet, and giant cracks radiated out from that spot.

Stupendous and the robot took turns lunging at each other, taking the occasional swing, looking for an opening. I pressed my face closer to the helicopter window until the battle was directly below us.

"We're right over them," Bobby said.

"Give me the filament," I said. "And get ready."

Bobby handed the filament canister over his shoulder.

"Hold up, Vincent," he said, handing over a clear plastic tube full of some kind of goo. "Strike this safety flare on the outside of the chopper to activate it, then drop it with the filament. Those things are extremely bright—Captain Stupendous can't miss seeing it."

DING, DING, DING! Thank you, Bobby! The

flare was totally gonna help, but not in the way Bobby thought.

I fumbled with the switch in my armrest, and the window zipped open, letting in a rush of air. Then I unbuckled my seat belt, which made a red light start flashing in the cockpit.

"We have an unsecured passenger," Silent Tom said.

"Wait, what are you doing, Vincent?" Bobby shouted.

"I have to lean out the window to make sure Stupendous sees me!" I lied.

"WHAT?"

"I have to!"

"Good grief . . . hold on, let's at least tie a rope around your waist so you don't fall out!"

Uh, no.

"Okay!" I lied again.

"Buckle up, Vincent! Be safe!"

I sighed, "Sure, Bobby."

I took a firm grip on the flare and filament canister. Then I closed my eyes, whacked the flare on my armrest, and tossed the flare between Bobby and Tom.

"VINCENT, NO!"

"AAARRRGH!"

"I SAID, 'OUTSIDE'!"

I kept my eyes closed, grabbed the edge of the window,

got my head and arms outside, where it was all *WHUP-WHUP-WHUP-WHUP*, and by thrashing my arms and kicking my feet I got the whole top half of my body outside.

Then I fell out of the helicopter.

CHAPTER

I regretted it right away, of course. No helicopter, no super-hero, just Vincent Wu dropping like a rock—it was total insanity! I couldn't tell if the whooshing in my ears was the helicopter, the wind, or just the sound of my panic. Once again, I was about to die.

Then Stupendous was there!

BAM! I yelped in pain as he caught me—we were going in opposite directions, after all. I almost cried with relief as Stupendous jetted away from the helicopter, which was going in slow circles above us.

"VINCENT! ARE YOU TRYING TO KILL YOURSELF?" Stupendous yelled in my ear, practically blowing out my eardrums.

"Oooooow, stop yelling in my ear!"

"Can't you see I'm BUSY? And you KNOW I hate helicopters!"

"Monofilament!" I said. "Carbon nanotube!"

"WHAT ARE YOU BABBLING ABOUT?"

Stupendous zigged and zagged across the sky, with Mayhem's robot hot on our tails.

"I have my dad's unbreakable fishing line!" I said. "If you get the robot to spin its arms around, you can use the fishing line to tangle it up like a gyroscope!"

I had the canister in a two-handed death grip, and I stuck it in his face.

"Get that thing out of my face!" Stupendous said. He accelerated into a big loop-de-loop over the robot's head and back toward the ground. The robot spun around, and we all stopped and hovered in midair.

Stupendous and I had our backs to the sun. We were right between the towers, and their shadows stretched forward on either side of us. The sunlight was all hazy and yellowish, and it lit up Mayhem's robot as it landed in the plaza again with a *CRUNCH*. I heard a faint *WHUP-WHUP-WHUP* sound from somewhere over us, and for a second I wondered if Bobby was okay.

"Tell me again about your dad's . . . what is it?" Stupendous said. "Magic string?"

I twisted open the canister and pulled out a shiny metal spool with a skinny black thread wrapped around its middle.

"Carbon nanotube monofilament," I said. "It's unbreakable, just like Mayhem's robot. Get it to do that helicopter thing with its upper body and *wind this string around its neck—*"

Stupendous looked at the canister, then busted out a huge, toothy, movie-star grin: the classic Captain Stupendous grin.

"Yeah," he said. "YEAH! Aw, he is toast."

Stupendous moved so fast that I didn't even see him grab the spool out of my hand. I went, "OOF," as he spun around, flew between the towers at light speed, and zoomed up over the top of them. He slowed down a little as we passed over the helicopter pad. My feet pinged and ricocheted off the pad, then Stupendous let me go. I tumbled a couple of times and slid to a halt.

Stupendous floated right over the center of the plaza, making big looping motions with his arms. I was too far away to see the monofilament, but I imagined it dangling from his hands in a big U shape, ready for a little robot destruction.

The robot raised its arms into a fighting pose, and Mayhem's voice yelled out.

"WHAT DO YOU HAVE THERE, STUPENDOUS?" Mayhem's voice said. "SOME KIND OF NEW TOY?"

"YOU'RE ABOUT TO FIND OUT," Stupendous

shouted. He rocketed around behind the robot's head and made a throwing motion. The sunlight reflected off a tiny metal object flying through the air—it was the monofilament spool.

ZOOM! Stupendous went into super-acceleration mode. The robot tried a spinning kick, but Stupendous dodged and flew in a circle around the robot's head. He stopped right in front of the robot's face and shouted at the top of his lungs.

"HEY, LOOOOOOOSER!"

"GRAAAAAAAHHHHHHRRRR!" Mayhem's voice said. The robot's arms went straight out from its body, and everything between its neck and waist blurred into motion. Stupendous got hit, but this time he wasn't sent flying like a baseball, because the robot's torso stopped spinning almost instantly.

There was a short, harsh *SKRINCH* sound as the robot's arms got tangled up in the monofilament. The robot's shoulders were pulled loose, its head jerked up at a weird angle, and its left arm caved in at the elbow. The robot actually smacked itself in the face with its own right hand, which knocked the head even farther back on its neck.

Game over, man.

"YEEEEAAAAAHHHH!" I hollered, and a faint cheer rose from the ground below. I ran to the edge and looked

cautiously over. The edges of the plaza were lined with people.

The robot hung there, arms and legs twitching, as Stupendous wrapped his arms around its bashed-in chin and planted one foot against its pushed-out shoulder. The muscles in his shoulders and arms bunched up as he slowly but surely twisted the robot's head around, then popped it all the way off. His momentum spun him partway around, but he hung on to the head with one hand and caught the headless body before it could hit the ground.

This time the cheering didn't stop, in fact it was more delirious screaming. Even from the top of the tallest building in Copperplate City I could hear it with no problem, and for a second I felt really alone. Then there was the sound of feet running across the roof behind me. I turned around just in time for Max and George to barrel into me, slapping me on the head and cackling like lunatics.

"YOU'RE ALIVE AGAIN!" Max yelled. He pumped both fists straight up in the air, over and over. George threw his head all the way back and laughed like a hyena.

I saw Security Guy Mendoza and some of his men step onto the roof behind Max and George, and I heard a gradually louder *WHUP-WHUP-WHUP* sound as Bobby's helicopter came down from the sky.

"Dude, you jumped out of a helicopter," Max said. "That was the craziest thing I've ever seen."

"It was the most AMAZING thing I've ever seen!" George said. "Did you get a spine transplant?"

"For a while I thought you were turning into the bravest kid ever, but now I know you just went nuts," Max said.

"You guys are just jealous," I said.

"Of you? No way," Max said.

Aw, geez. Ow.

"Of course not," I said, feeling like I'd just had my three-ring binder knocked out of my hands in the school hallway. "Who'd be jealous of—"

"Dude, no," Max said, and all of a sudden his voice was dead serious. "What I mean is—I just—look at it this way: Name one other kid in history who's ever made it through *three* supervillain attacks, then *defeated the villain.* Bet you can't do it."

I tried, and Max was right. "Can't do it."

"See? What I mean is when you're in the Captain Stupendous Fan Club, you can't be jealous of El Presidente. And that's you, Vincent."

I wasn't gonna be all gross and say so, but I felt a happy, little *zing!* when Max said that. He held up a fist, so I made my hand into a fist, looked at it, and bumped Max's fist with it. Max grinned as George and I smacked our fists together, then we all did a ridiculous group guy-hug. I almost lost my balance, but the guys kept me from falling over.

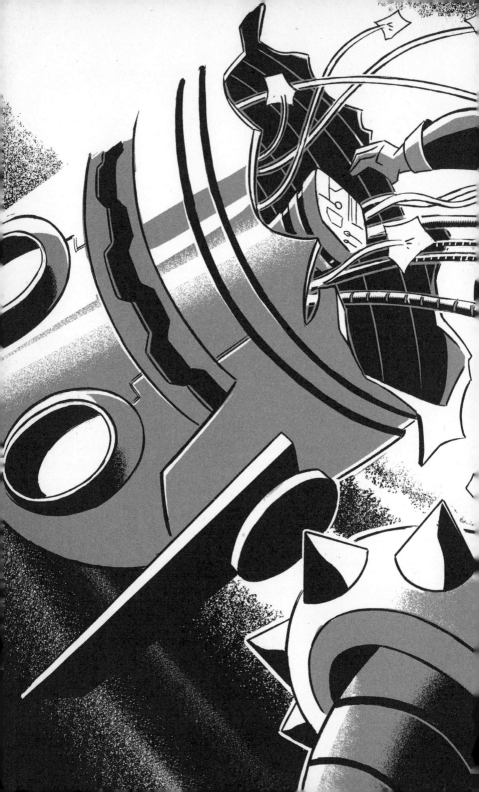

Everybody else arrived on the roof at the same time—Bobby and Silent Tom from the helicopter, Mom, Dad, and Janet Corwin from the stairwell. Mom and Dad looked ready to tear my head off my shoulders, or Bobby's head, or both.

Most importantly, Captain Stupendous arrived.

I turned back toward the plaza just in time to see him rise over the edge of the rooftop, carrying the robot head like a suitcase. He flew in nice and slow and dropped the head, which put a big ding in the roof when it landed. There was still enough reddish-orange light in the sky to reflect off the robot's eyeballs. The sky was full of long, streaky clouds, as if a bunch of fighter planes had just zoomed off into the sunset.

Stupendous ripped the robot's face off. There was an "oooh" from the small rooftop crowd—not everyone had as much experience seeing Stupendous in action as I did. Stupendous tossed the robot face over his shoulder with a *CLUNK*, dragged Professor Mayhem out by the front of his lab coat, and dropped him on the cement in a pile of elbows and knees.

"Okay, freak, they're gonna lock you up now," Stupendous said. "Maybe somebody can figure out why you're so totally crazy."

Mayhem laughed, then snorted. Blood ran down his

cheek, and he pressed one hand lightly against his temple.

"Oh, and for your information, I know at least TWENTY girls who could knock your sorry butt into the next state!" Stupendous leaned down and pointed one huge finger right at Mayhem's nose as he spoke. "YOU SUCK, AND GIRLS ARE AWESOME."

Mayhem blinked. "What are you *on* about, you thyroidal cretin?" he said.

Bobby went right up to Professor Mayhem as a whole mess of cops came out of the stairwells and onto the roof. There must have been at least twenty of them.

"Captain Stupendous, I think we can hang on to Professor Mayhem until Villain Containment Services arrives," Bobby said. "We've already called them."

"Uh, okay, that sounds good," Stupendous said. "Thanks."

Bobby nodded. He jerked his head at the other cops, and they swarmed over Mayhem, cuffing his hands behind his back.

"GET HIM OUT OF HERE," Bobby thundered.

"VIOLET!" Mayhem shouted. "VIOLET, THIS IS NOT OVER! UNHAND ME, DOLTS!"

Mayhem kicked hard and swung his body from side to side as the cops hauled him off. I knew from experience how strong he was, but twenty cops are twenty cops.

Bobby spun on one foot and walked over to George, Max, and me. He looked pissed off—can you get arrested for blinding a cop and jumping out of a helicopter? I was a little scared, but then he gave me a crooked, little smile and a wink.

"That's some stunt you pulled, Vincent," he said.

Stupendous walked up next to Bobby.

"Hey, Officer, can I talk to these . . . uh, these kids?" he said. "In private?"

"Of course, Captain," Bobby said.

Bobby pulled out his walkie-talkie and hustled over to the cops who were manhandling Professor Mayhem down the stairs.

So there we were, just the four of us—Captain Stupendous and the Captain Stupendous Fan Club, the center of attention, just like I'd always dreamed, except my knees had practically no skin on them and I had puke on my shoes.

Stupendous smiled, and slowly stuck out his hand in my direction.

I peeked at George and Max on either side, but neither of them had their hands out. So I stuck mine out instead, and Stupendous wrapped his big, old, gloved hand around my hand and shook it.

"Thanks," he said. "I couldn't have done it without—"

Stupendous snapped his mouth closed and looked up.

He had these deep shadows under his eyes, nose, and chin, which was strange because the sunset was coming from the wrong direction for shadows like that. But something in the sky was giving off more and more light.

Blue light, to be exact.

I don't know how a giant spaceship sneaks up on a whole city, but this one did—it must have come down through the atmosphere really fast. It was an old-school flying saucer. The flattened-out saucer section spun slowly, just like in the old monster movies on TV, while the middle section stayed still. The blue light came from a strip along the bottom of the saucer section. Mayhem's robot made Captain Stupendous look like a doll, but the flying saucer made Mayhem's robot look like a prize you'd get from a cereal box. Everyone craned their necks back.

The spaceship stopped a few hundred feet above us, although it was hard to tell for sure because it was so unbelievably huge. It made no sound—I could hear people on the rooftop talking, and from way down below I thought I heard a *CRASH*, like somebody getting into a car accident.

A circular spot on the bottom of the flying saucer turned bright blue, and at the same second, a wide cylinder of blue light appeared around the four of us. It was like a cone of silence was slapped down over us—all the noise from the people and the wind and everything was cut off. A breathy female voice started talking.

"This is the Grakkian Interdimensional Envoy Vehicle for Dimension 22GWP, Planet XX45, self-identified as 'Earth,'" the breathy voice said.

"What did it say?" Max said. I elbowed him in the side.

"You are Test Subject LLVU744192, self-identified as 'Captain Stupendous'?"

Stupendous looked at me, and I shrugged. He looked back up at the ship.

"I guess," he said.

"According to our submolecular wave scans, your native biological matrix has changed."

"I don't know what that means," Stupendous said.

"You are not Miguel Zazueta, the original recruit this artificial matrix was designed for."

George, Max, and I jumped and looked around—stupid aliens, coming right out and revealing his secret identity!

"You are contained within a sonic modulation emission," the alien voice said. "This interactive episode cannot be monitored by external life-forms."

"What?" Max said.

"Nobody can hear us," I said, pointing with my thumb at the other people on the roof. I caught a glimpse of Mom standing next to Bobby.

"You are not Miguel Zazueta," the alien voice said.

Stupendous opened his mouth, then closed it.

"No, I'm not," Stupendous said. "Can you use a different voice? One that's less annoying?"

"This was the voice chosen for this liaison unit by Miguel Zazueta."

"Good choice," Max said under his breath.

"Who are you?" I said. I guess I said it kinda loud, because Stupendous, Max, and George all turned to look at me.

"This is the Grakkian Interdimensional Envoy Vehicle for Dimension 22GWP, Planet XX45, self-identified as 'Earth.'"

"What's a Grakkian?" I said.

I guess the aliens were done with dumb, old non-super-powered Vincent, because they totally ignored me.

"Recruit, the Grakkian High Command nearly decommissioned your artificial matrix due to performance irregularities," the voice said. "Your subsequent performance has confirmed that decommissioning your matrix is unnecessary, but you must undergo a secondary course of orientation and redeployment processes.

"Prepare for submolecular transport."

"What do you mean, transport? What's going on?" Stupendous said.

"Redeployment?" I said. "Is that like reassignment?"

"Do you think I know, Vincent?" Stupendous said.

"Can you guys use shorter words?" Max said, holding his head with both hands. "Seriously."

"Associate life-forms have been included in extended communications due to their role in the recently concluded engagement with the assailant life-form. Extended communications will now be terminated. Associate life-forms will remain on Dimension 22GWP, Planet XX45," the voice said. "Initiate."

"WAIT!" I shouted, but the shaft of light surrounding us instantly shrank so it was just around Stupendous. The sounds, smells, and heat of the regular world washed over us all at once. Stupendous looked at me for a second, but snapped his eyes back up. Stupendous said something, but we only saw his lips moving. I tried to touch his arm—he was standing right next to me—but my hand wouldn't go into the shaft of light.

There we were, the Captain Stupendous Fan Club. We were at the scene of an epic, victorious battle, bathed in spooky blue light from a Grakkian interdimensional cruiser, with our idol looking right at us. It was like our craziest, geekiest fan-boy dream come true. And it was messed up. It sucked. It felt terrible. After everything we'd done to help Stupendous—to help Polly—we were helpless.

Stupendous looked at us. The blue light made his already

glistening hair glisten even more. He said something else we couldn't hear. I spread my hands apart, Max put one hand behind his ear, and George shook his head.

Stupendous shut his mouth and did that making-his-hands-into-claws thing in front of his face. He held out one hand in our direction, palm facing down, took a deep breath, and tried again, exaggerating his mouth movements. It looked like he was saying "I'LL . . . BE . . ."

But we didn't find out what he'd be, because the tube of light around him flared and got sparkly. Then FLASH, the light got superbright, then supersparkly, then it spun round and round and went off like a firecracker. When the light went out there was an empty place where Captain Stupendous had been.

The ship floated there for a few seconds, then the saucer section spun faster and faster until it was a glowing blur. The ship accelerated straight up, *BAMF*. The air swirled and whooshed around us as the ship became the size of a basketball, then a Ping-Pong ball, then a speck, then nothing at all.

Captain Stupendous was gone.

Polly was gone.

I stood there, blinking, with a stupid lump in my throat. George crossed his arms and bit his thumbnail, and Max laced both hands behind his head. Our mouths were all sealed up tight, and I saw Max's throat clench as he swallowed.

"Is he coming back?" George said.

"I don't know," I said, and with a manly effort I kept my voice from cracking.

Nobody moved for a long time. Eventually I heard a few people come our way, but I kept looking at the sky, so I didn't know one of them was Mom until she appeared in front of me and wrapped me up in a big hug without saying anything. She smelled a little bit flowery, and she pressed one hand against the back of my neck.

She let go, and Dad came out of nowhere and hugged me too. He came at me sideways, so my left arm got pinned between us. I felt his glasses dig briefly into my scalp, but he shifted and pressed his cheek against the top of my head. He hugged me even longer than Mom had. I felt a puff of his breath against my forehead, and for a second I almost cried. I didn't, but it was close.

Mom put her hands on my shoulders.

"Don't you ever do anything like that again," she said. "Flying right into the middle of a Captain Stupendous battle? You could have been killed!"

"Mom, I helped catch Professor Mayhem!" I said. I looked at Max and George for a little moral support. They'd both taken one big step away from me during the hugging part, but they came crowding back in next to me. George gave me a thumbs-up, and Max actually bumped into Mom.

"Boys, please," Mom said.

"Vincent's the man, Ms. Keller," Max said in a serious voice—not his partly fake, partly real deep voice, but a *serious* serious voice. "He's a hero."

"Yeah, he's El Presidente!" George said. He stood up really straight, almost as straight as Bobby, and his jaw was clenched.

"Your mother's right," Dad said, ignoring the guys. "Captain Stupendous is superhuman, but you're just a boy."

"Just a boy." One of the most evil three-word phrases in the English language. I could feel my head getting ready to burst into flames when Bobby walked up.

"And you!" Mom said, glaring at Bobby. She and Dad both straightened up and put their hands on their hips, like they were doing a really lame dance. "Putting Vincent in harm's way like that, what were you thinking?"

"He didn't give me much choice, Violet," Bobby said.

"You're a police officer, Bobby," Mom said.

Bobby sighed and looked at me.

"They're right, you know," Bobby said. "You took an enormous risk."

"I had to tell him about the plan," I said.

"You told me he already knew."

"I lied."

I don't usually just admit to lying like that, and I halfway expected Bobby to answer me with his own version of Mom's I-will-destroy-you voice. But he just started chuckling.

"Bobby?" Mom said, and she did use her I-will-destroy-you voice.

"Is there something funny going on here?" Dad said, straightening his dirty glasses.

"I'm sorry," Bobby said. He kept chuckling, though. "Your son reminds me of myself at his age, but he's much more brave and resourceful than I was."

Say what?

"Vincent, you just helped Captain Stupendous catch a genuine, no-doubt-about-it supervillain," Bobby said. "I dreamed about doing the exact same thing when I was in the Official Captain Stupendous Fan Club years ago."

Bobby used to be an Official? Holy cow, who else was secretly a Captain Stupendous fan? The mayor? Mom? My cat?

Bobby stuck out his hand. "Thanks. We couldn't have done it without you."

I looked him right in the eye, then I slowly reached out and shook his hand.

"We'll talk about this later, Bobby," Mom said, and I could tell from her voice that it wasn't gonna be a fun talk.

"Vincent," Dad said. "I—"

He took his glasses off and rubbed his face.

"I still think you were reckless. But your solution to the robot problem . . . was an intelligent one."

"Thanks, Dad," I said. "You know what, Professor Mayhem bragged a lot about how much smarter he is than you, but your invention beat his invention."

Dad smiled. I could tell he was trying not to, because he only smiled with one side of his mouth, but the other side twitched a couple of times.

"I suppose so," he said in a soft voice. "I feel a little sorry for him, though. Dennis was . . . *is* a brilliant mind. He could have done great things. Such a waste."

"I guess." Mayhem spewed a lot of crazy talk while we were in his underwater lair, but I felt a little sorry for him too. Not TOO much—he was a psycho, after all—but a little.

Mom put a hand gently on my cheek, and suddenly I was tired. My head hurt, Polly was gone, and I just wanted to go to bed.

"Can we go home?" I said.

"Sure," Mom said. Dad pulled a handkerchief out of his pocket and started polishing his glasses, looking down at them while he did it. Dad always looks a little lost to me without his glasses, like he's trying to see where he's going but can't really.

Mom looked at the guys. "Max? George? We'll take you home too."

The guys and I looked at each other, and we had another one of those rare moments when we have nothing to say. So we just looked up at the sky one more time.

For a second I thought I saw the Grakkian ship way off in the distance, but it could have been a shooting star, or a superhero flying home from some other galaxy. Then the last bits of sunlight went away and all I saw was a dark sky, with a few stars scattered around, and nothing that flew, not even a bird.

CHAPTER

Helping the most super superhero in the world take down the baddest bad guy in the world was pretty much the most exciting time of my life. The next forty-eight hours were probably the most . . . I guess "boring" isn't the right word, just because of the teddy bear thing. Teddy bears started disappearing from people's houses and showing up in random places all over town. A whole bunch of them were found piled up in front of city hall. The news made it sound like somebody was just playing a really complicated practical joke, but it made me wonder if a new villain was already scoping out Copperplate City.

So I couldn't get very bored because I was too busy being stressed out by the idea of a new bad guy showing up while Stupendous was gone. In the meantime, Bobby took statements from me, the guys, Mom, and Dad. I went to see the doctor, and I was there so long getting x-rayed and poked and mangled that it felt more like going to jail. Reporters hovered around the house like wingless vultures; Mom even had a yelling match with one of them, which was fun to listen to, even if I had to stay in the back of the house so no one would take my picture.

Mom also took some vacation time! Oh, the horror! It was cool when she was ambushing reporters, but after all that stuff died down she insisted on spending quality time together to help us both get over all our near-death experiences. We talked about how mad she was at Bobby. We talked about Dad. We talked about how I shouldn't jump out of helicopters anymore, even if it worked out okay this time. We talked and talked and talked, and after twenty-four hours of non-stop Mom time, I was ready to hit myself in the face with a hammer. So the next morning she read magazines while I watched TV. That afternoon she went shopping while I rode my bike slowly up and down the block. That night we got fried chicken for dinner and went to a movie. The day after that she went back to work, and I went back to the fan club.

When we started talking about the teddy bear situation, it sank in that Captain Stupendous was somewhere in a galaxy far, far away. There was plenty of stuff in the news about Stupendous, Mayhem, and the spaceship, but it was all from the fight at Corwin Towers. We spent a lot of time in the garage reading science fiction, eating junk food, and monitoring the TV for Stupendous news and stuffed-animal sightings. Every once in a while we'd talk about a book, or some TV show, or about how unfair it was that school was open the day after Professor Mayhem was caught instead of staying closed for another week. And every once in a LONG while we'd toss around theories about where Polly was, and what it meant that she said "I'll be—" just before disappearing, but it never lasted long. We kept our eyes on the news for any mention of Polly's disappearance, but there was nothing at all.

Five days after the final battle I was hanging out in the driveway, not really wanting to be in club headquarters by myself, when Max and George coasted in on their bikes. Max dropped his bike loudly on the pavement.

"Dude, you know you can't just leave that thing in the middle of our driveway," I said.

"Don't worry, Vincent, I'll pick it up," Max said, without doing anything to make you think he actually would pick it up. He picked a random stick off the ground instead and swung it around like a baseball bat, while George leaned his bike against the garage wall.

"How long's it been?" Max said.

"Since the aliens took Captain Stupendous, you mean?" George said.

"No, I mean since the aliens abducted your brain, George," Max said.

"Dude, why the rage?" George said. "Geez."

"Five days," I said. "It's been forever."

I stared out over the fence at the big hill covered in eucalyptus trees a few blocks over—Skyside Park, where Polly landed the day that Mom was kidnapped.

"You really think there's a new villain in town?" George said.

"I hope not." Max took a vicious uppercut swing with his stick, then tossed it over his shoulder. "A villain whose big weapon is teddy bears? How lame would that be?"

"Geppetto the Destroyer wasn't lame." I kicked at a weed growing from a crack in the cement.

"Geppetto used giant puppets with rocket launchers in their chests," Max said, "not a bunch of stuffed bears."

"Yeah, but it started the same way, with that puppet show at the Luthor Hall of Science coming to life."

"We should ask Bobby what he thinks," George said.

"I think my mom was talking to him about it last night on the phone."

"Bobby's a good guy," Max said. "He's a mensch, you know? That means he's a good guy."

"Yeah, Max, we figured out what 'mensch' means after the first eight hundred times you said it." I patted Max on the shoulder.

"Bobby's awesome, are you kidding?" George said. "He believed us, for one thing."

"He also gave us the greatest helicopter ride ever," Max said.

"Yeah, I know," I said. "I'm not used to *liking* my mom's boyfriend, though."

"I don't like any of my mom's boyfriends." George shrugged. "It sucks, dude, you should be psyched."

"Your mom could have a boyfriend like my dad, Vincent," Max said. "Your house would smell like smoke and rotten ham sandwiches."

"I know, I know, I'm just not used to it."

"It's a good thing to get used to," George said. "Trust me."

A dog barked somewhere in the distance, and a few houses over I heard a car door slam, followed by angry-sounding voices. That made me think of Polly, of course.

"Polly really is as tough as she seems, huh?"

"That is so cool that she kicked Mayhem in the solar plexus!" George grinned.

"I don't get tough girls," I said.

Max ran his hands through his hair and leaned back with his elbows on the steps behind him.

"What's there to get?" he said. "They're *girls*, they're just, you know, different."

"You're the big expert, huh?" I said.

"I am," Max said, intentionally making his voice as deep as possible.

"It's not just the tough girls!" George threw his hands up in the air. "I don't understand any of them!"

"Seriously, regular girls are weird enough, but what do you say to a girl who could beat you up?" I said.

Max and George both cracked up a little, and Max slapped me on the shoulder.

"I don't know, Vincent," he said. "How about 'hi'? Or 'my name's Vincent'?"

"Just 'hi' and nothing else?"

"Do you like Polly? I mean, do you LIKE, like her?" George said.

"No!" I crossed my arms.

"Why not?" Max said.

"We don't care, you know," George said. "It's awesome!"

"Polly's okay, Vincent," Max said. "What's the big deal, anyway?"

"You don't think it'd be kind of a big deal if, you know . . ."

"I'm just saying, it wouldn't be a big deal to me. We'd still hang out." Max socked me on the shoulder, but for once he didn't do it very hard.

"Do you think she's coming back?" George said.

"She's coming back," I said. "She HAS to, especially if there really is a new villain in town."

"She's totally coming back, Vincent," Max said. "I'm going inside, it's getting hot out here."

"Me too," George said.

"You guys go in, I'll be there in a minute."

I unlocked the door, and after Max and George went inside I walked back to the steps and stared at the eucalyptus trees some more. I really like that eucalyptus smell—it's a little bit smoky and a little bit spicy. I was imagining that smell in my head when the wind kicked up. A few of the treetops jerked and swayed, a handful of leaves scattered into the air, and I realized it wasn't the wind, because the rest of the trees didn't move at all. It was a sunny October day, so the flash of blue light might have been my imagination, but I knew it wasn't. I *knew* it. My heart started pumping really fast, and it wasn't all *lub-DUB, lub-DUB* like they say in school. It was more like *WHAMWHAMWHAMWHAMWHAMWHAMWHAM!*

I ran to the garage and stuck my head inside.

"Skyside Park!"

Max did his flailing-arms thing and knocked a magazine right out of George's hands. George got halfway to his feet.

"What about Skyside Park?" Max said.

"STUPENDOUS ALERT!" I screamed.

George and Max burst out of their chairs, hollering like lunatics. We stampeded out of the garage, hopped onto our bikes, and hit the road in about thirty seconds flat. The five blocks between my house and Skyside Park felt like five feet, and we were on the park's main trail and halfway up the hill before we realized how incredibly steep it actually is. Man, it is really steep—no wonder I could see it so easily from my house. We got off our bikes and started walking them when Max reached over and grabbed George's arm.

"Hey, George, let's wait here," he said. We hadn't reached the crest of the hill yet, so all we could see were the tops of the trees up ahead.

"What are you talking about?" I said.

"Yeah, what ARE you talking about?" George said. "I wanna go up there too!"

"Let's give Vincent a little privacy," Max said.

George looked at Max, then at me. Then he grinned, a big, old, goofy George grin.

"Yeah, okay," he said. "We'll be here, Vincent."

"You're not coming?" I said, feeling confused.

"Dude," Max said. "How dense are you? We'll wait here."

"Oh," I said. "OH. Uh, yeah, okay."

I turned away from the guys, which felt a little weird, and pushed my bike up over the crest of the hill.

The smell of the eucalyptus trees hit me as I lay my bike down on the path, and I sucked in a big lungful when Polly stepped out from behind a tree and made a tiny waving motion. I took a half step, stopped, then started again. We met just outside the line of trees. She wore a plain white T-shirt and jeans, a black messenger bag over her shoulder, and a smile that showed the gap between her front teeth. I got a little dizzy when she stuck her arms under mine, squeezed me around the chest, and pressed her face hard into my shoulder. At first I held my arms up like a scarecrow, but eventually I put an arm around her neck and the other arm on top of that arm.

We snapped out of it after a few seconds. Polly stepped back and crossed her arms, with one shoulder pushed up higher than the other, and I put my hands down by my sides, then in my front pockets, then in my back pockets.

"Hey," she said.

"You look really tired," I said.

"Geez, Vincent, you sure know how dish up a compliment."

"No, I just meant—you know, things have been kind of messed up. That's all."

"Messed up is right. I was on a Grakkian interdimensional cruiser getting trained to be a superhero, you know."

"The cops put out one of those missing kid reports on you a couple of days ago."

"They did, huh?"

"My mom's boyfriend was the one who talked to your mom about it," I said.

"Detective Carpenter?" Polly said. "I talked to him too. He's an okay guy."

"When did you talk to Bobby?"

"I actually got home yesterday."

"What did you tell him? Not the truth, right?"

"I said I got picked up by the same UFO that took Stupendous, the aliens ran all these bizarre tests on me, and they dropped me off on the edge of town."

"That's genius! A thousand other people are claiming the same thing, there's no way to disprove it!"

"Yeah, well, I don't know if he believed me."

"That doesn't matter, you're good as long as you don't change your story."

I was so happy to see her! Yeah, I know, that's gross and

weird, but there she was, gap toothed, short, and fresh off an alien spaceship. Max was right, I had a GIGANTIC crush on her. Rats. I swallowed hard.

"Ummm, hey, I don't know if I told you before, but I, uh, I like you."

I wasn't nervous, just so you know. My forehead was sweating, and my neck was itchy, and I couldn't figure out what to do with my stupid hands, but nervous? Who, me?

"I like you too, Vincent."

"I mean, um, well, I LIKE, like you."

"Oh." Polly made an exaggerated O shape with her mouth, looked down, and smiled.

"Maybe we should, I don't know, go to the movies?" I said.

"Sure," Polly said. "Or we could save the world or something like that."

"Yeah. Something like that."

We looked at the ground for a while. Polly swept a few leaves to the side with the side of one foot, and I used one of my feet to poke around the shoelace on my other foot. I tilted my head up and looked at Polly out of the corner of my eye. She was looking at me from under her eyebrows, and we both looked down again.

". . . Um," I said.

I scratched my neck and finally just looked at Polly.

"The guys are waiting down there," I said. I stuck my thumb over my shoulder.

"Yeah, I figured," Polly said. "I'm kind of glad you came up here first."

"Me too," I said.

Polly looked up and smiled, a big, big smile. She hauled my hand out of my pocket by the elbow, held it in her hand, then hooked her other hand under the strap of her messenger bag.

"Let's go. I have some stuff to tell you guys."

Of course I had to let go of her hand to pick up my bike, but it was pretty cool to hold hands with a girl for twenty feet or so. I had no idea how sweaty your hand gets when you hold someone else's hand, though—when I picked up my bike I secretly wiped my hand on my shirt so Polly wouldn't see.

It turned out Max and George were slooooowly making their way up the hill anyway, so we ran into them about three seconds later. Polly hugged both of them too, although she also socked Max on the arm. George shouted, "AWESOME!" two or three times, which was a little nerve-racking because people were starting to show up in the park and a couple of them looked our way.

"George, you nutcase, let's keep a low profile," I said. "We gotta protect Polly's secret identity, remember?" And just because I was feeling like nothing in the galaxy could embarrass me at that moment, I reached over and held Polly's hand again. She even let me.

"Oh right!" George said, not looking like he cared much. "LOW PROFILE!"

"We better get back to headquarters before George blows a gasket," Max said. He looked at my hand holding Polly's hand.

"Mazel tov," he said with a huge grin. He turned to George. "That means 'congrats on the awesome stuff you've got going on,' just so you know."

"I know what 'mazel tov' means, Dad," George said. "You have actually been Jewish the whole time I've known you."

When we got to the bottom of the hill we saw a handful of other kids coming toward the park. It was Scott Fanelli and his tribe of morons, cackling loudly about something and swaggering along like usual.

"Hey, it's the Unofficial Captain Stupendous Loser Club!" Scott said. "What are—" He trailed off when I let go of my bike's handlebar and held Polly's hand, which she'd already held out in my direction. Scott looked back up at my face with his mouth open, and I looked him right in the eye without saying a word.

It was fantastic.

One of Scott's caveman followers thumped him on the back of his shoulder. Scott coughed.

"So, hey, Polly, how about you ditch these rejects and hang out with us?" Scott gave Polly his usual irritating grin, but his eyes darted down to our hands again.

"No."

Polly's "no" was so totally pure and simple, I couldn't help breaking out in a cheesy grin of my own. For the first time ever, I saw Scott Fanelli lose his cool. His eyebrows knotted up, his face turned pink, and the corners of his mouth turned down. I guess he wasn't used to not getting his way.

"Okay, whatever. We're just gonna check out some confidential info about Professor Mayhem's origin story, but if you want to miss out on—"

We burst out laughing—I mean, we totally lost it. Scott and his buddies shuffled their feet and crossed their arms as we laughed and laughed and laughed.

"Dude, he's right! We're so gonna miss out!" George said.

"Where did you get this so-called confidential info?" I said, gasping for breath.

"Right, like I'm gonna give up our sources," Scott said. His face wasn't pink anymore, it was bright, stop-sign red. "You losers wouldn't know anything about how to get info on a villain like Profess—"

"Oh no, we don't know squat about that," Polly said, which cracked us up again.

Max closed his eyes and howled, his big shoulders shaking and his tongue hanging out. George bent over and clutched himself around the middle as he laughed. Polly threw her head back and shrieked laughter at the sky, her hair falling behind her like a short, shimmery wave. The muscles in my face and stomach started to hurt.

"Let's go," I said. Still laughing, we walked right through Scott and his goon squad. Scott had to scramble to get out of my and Polly's way, and Max went shoulder to shoulder with one of the nameless goons. The goon staggered back from the impact, and George stared him down as we went by and continued down the hill.

"I brought food," Polly said when we were safely back at HQ. She slung the messenger bag on the table and opened it, revealing a stash of quality junk food.

"So the aliens have junk food on their interdimensional cruiser, huh?" Max said.

"NO, they don't have junk food, although they could probably make it," Polly said. "I went to the store before I came here."

"Was your mom going totally bananas?" I said.

"She's *still* going bananas," Polly said. "For a while after I got back I thought she was just gonna chain me to the kitchen table 24/7, and she's making me go to a shrink because of the alien abduction story." She sighed. "I hate going to therapy."

"There must have been a million reporters at your house," George said.

"Nope," Polly said. "Mom said the news was nothing but Captain Stupendous while I was gone. She was pissed off about that, actually."

"What about your dad?" Max said.

Polly shrugged. "He's in India for some work thing—Mom said we should wait until he gets back before we tell him about it."

"That's about fourteen varieties of lame," George said. Max and I nodded.

Polly shrugged again, then spread her hands apart with her fingers wide open in a showtime kind of gesture. "That's my dad."

"Maybe nobody's made the connection," Max said. "Between Polly and Captain Stupendous, I mean."

"Maybe not," Polly said.

"Probably not," I said. "And the reporters can't interview everyone who says they were kidnapped by the UFO."

We got comfortable in our chairs and chowed on doughnuts, beef jerky, and honey-mustard pretzel nuggets. George and Max put their feet up on the table.

"So what's it like hanging out with aliens?" Max said, sliding way down low in his chair.

"You were on a spaceship!" George said. "It must have been the most amazing thing ever, huh?"

"'Amazing' is not even the word," Polly said.

"So what's the deal?" I couldn't wait any longer. "How did Mr. Zazueta become Captain Stupendous? Was it the meteorite?"

Polly nodded. "Yup. See, the Grakkians are an interdimensional peacekeeping force. They recruit people on all these different worlds and dimensions, and make superpowered bodies for them to fight with."

"So they're like cops for the entire universe," I said.

"Pretty much," Polly said. "But they'd never recruited someone on this planet before—they only tried it with Mr. Zazueta because one of their ships was damaged during an interdimensional jump, and he was hit by a piece of the transmogrification matrix."

"So my dad and Professor Mayhem both found pieces of a Grakkian ship. Wow. So when your Stupendous body got all lit up and glowy during the battle at my mom's office, was that them?"

"Yeah," Polly said. "They did a remote scan to see what was going on."

"You're a soldier?" George said.

"No way," Max said. "You hate it when people tell you what to do, and soldiers are *always* told what to do."

"It's not really like being a soldier," Polly said.

"Don't they know Earth has fifty-seven known superheroes operating right now?" Max said.

"Fifty-two," George said.

"Whatever," Max said.

"There weren't so many superheroes twenty-five years ago," I pointed out.

"And none of the other superheroes are as good as Captain Stupendous, right?" Polly said.

"Right!" George said.

"Technically I'm supposed to patrol the whole planet, but with all those other superheroes I don't need to, not unless something comes up that no other superhero can handle," Polly said.

"But what about 'oh, nobody asked me if I wanted to do this,' and all that?" Max asked.

Polly shrugged.

"Maybe because nobody asked Mr. Zazueta if he wanted to be Captain Stupendous either, but he did it anyway."

"And he ROCKED as a superhero," I said.

Polly smiled. "Yeah. And, I don't know . . . he was, like, my mentor or something, right?"

We all nodded.

"Lots of superheroes had mentors when they started out," Max said.

"Captain Stupendous never had one." George shook his head.

"Until now!" I said, smiling at Polly. She smiled back, and I felt a little bit warm and tingly when she did. It was totally different being smiled at by a girl who's maybe sort of your girlfriend.

"That's awesome! It's kind of like how I'm Vincent's and George's mentor," Max said. Whatever he said next was drowned out by all the boos and snorting from everyone else.

Polly told us about Earth food on the Grakkian interdimensional cruiser (terrible, all soy based), the Grakkian noninvasive neural feed (tiring, but not painful), and what Grakkians look like (a mix between people, hippos, and turtles).

"Are you gonna tell your parents you're Captain Stupendous?" George said.

Polly snorted.

"NO," she said. "Are you kidding? It's hard enough to get out of the house as it is!"

"What did you tell them?" I said.

"Same thing I told the cops," Polly said.

"I guess now you know everything you need to know

about being Captain Stupendous, huh?" Max said, sounding a little sad.

The tone of Max's voice threw me into a minor panic. *Maybe she doesn't need us anymore!*

"No way," Polly said, shaking her head. I relaxed and slid lower in my chair.

"I don't know where Captain Stupendous's . . . where *my* secret headquarters is. There probably is one, right?"

Everybody nodded.

"Probably an incredible one," George said.

"I also don't know about all the villains out there, or the other superheroes, or the research labs and all that stuff you guys DO know."

"True, very true," Max said.

"I guess you're stuck with us," I said.

"I guess we're stuck with each other," Polly said.

"So are we your official sidekicks now?" George said.

"No," Polly said.

That was not what we wanted to hear.

"WHY NOT?" "WHAT'S YOUR PROBLEM, POLLY?" "THAT IS SO UNFAIR!" "YOU SUCK!" "WHAT, ARE YOU TOO GOOD FOR US NOW?"

"SHUT UP!" Polly yelled.

We quieted down, but the room was full of crossed arms and mopey expressions.

"What is this crap about sidekicks?" Polly said. "We're a *team*, you dummies! All of us!"

Suddenly the room was full of uncrossed arms and dopey grins.

"Oh!" George said. "That's different!"

"Actually, we're a club," Max said.

"Yeah, yeah, sure," Polly said. "Wait, I still have to tell you one more thing."

Polly put her hands on the edge of the table, pushed her chair back, and stood up. That gap-toothed smile was on her face again.

"Vincent, you were right about the thing with the inter-dimensional holding tank. That's exactly what happens when I switch bodies."

I put my hands up in the air and swiveled in my seat to face the guys, who immediately threw pretzel chunks at my head.

"The Grakkians said it's important for the Stupendous body to be exactly the way I want it," Polly said. "They use this thing called a subatomic particle alignment chamber to make the Stupendous body. So I told them to get rid of the old superhero body Mr. Zazueta designed and make one that I like."

Polly put her hands over her mouth, winked at me, and said something we couldn't hear.

ZOOP! As expected, there was a globe of fiery blue light. It hung there for a second, throwing off little tentacles of light, and then it blipped out. We blinked like crazy and rubbed our eyes to get rid of the afterglow. When I opened my eyes, Captain Stupendous was standing there: five foot two, black hair, dark blue costume and cape, looking about twelve years old. Yep, there she was, Captain Stupendous.

Yeah, you heard me right. SHE!

Captain Stupendous wasn't a hulking, steroid-looking guy with wavy black hair, bronze skin, big teeth, and arms the size of telephone poles anymore. Captain Stupendous was . . . well, Polly. With a costume and a mask.

"Wow," George said. "I mean, wow. Really."

"WHAT?" Max said. "HOW DID . . . WHEN . . . WHAT?"

This totally threw off my system of mentally separating Polly and Captain Stupendous to avoid gender confusion. I could call them both "she" and "her" now. So confusing! The thing that was confusing before just became less confusing, which actually made things even more confusing!

Polly smiled, and I noticed one difference in the way she looked. She caught my eye and tapped her two front teeth.

"No gap," she said. "For secret identity purposes."

I tapped my temple.

"Brains."

"That's right."

"But, wait, what . . . that other body was awesome! The arms! And the muscles! And the tallness!" George said.

Polly folded her arms and raised an eyebrow.

"This one is so much better," she said.

And you know what, she was right.

"You still have all the powers, right?" I said.

Polly nodded.

"What are you gonna call yourself?" Max said.

"Captain Stupendous."

"Really?" George said.

"Yeah, really. What's wrong with it?"

"It's gonna confuse everyone on the entire planet."

"The entire planet better get used to it."

I liked the change. Dark blue boots, silky cape, slightly darker blue costume—it was a whole new look. She even had a new logo on her chest, a spiky *S* with no *C*.

"You look good," Max said.

"You look awesome," George said.

"You look stupendous," I said.

Everyone groaned, but I didn't care.

"So, Captain, there's this situation going on," Max said.

"With potentially evil bears," George said, nodding his head seriously.

Max and George started giving Polly the deets on the teddy

bear weirdness, and before joining in I took a minute to, you know, stop and smell the roses. It was a good day to be Vincent Wu. My mom was safe; I had the best friends a guy could want; I had a date with a cute girl who also happened to be the most powerful superhero in history; and I belonged to the smallest, dorkiest, greatest fan club in the world.

There are still four Captain Stupendous fan clubs in Copperplate City, but don't even waste your time with the other three. We're the only one that's ever brought down a grade-A bad guy. We're the only one that knows the full story on the new and improved Stupendous. And we're the only one with a real live superhero IN the club. We're ready to flex the skinny biceps of justice whenever evildoers come around, whether they're supernatural boogeymen; pissed-off, foreign demigods; or sixth-grade bullies. We may be the smallest fan club in the city—maybe in the country, possibly on the entire planet—but we're the real deal.

We're the Captain Stupendous Fan Club, yo, and we are twenty-two varieties of awesome. All together now—
Stupendous Alert!

THE

END

ACKNOWLEDGMENTS

Arthur Levine is the quintessential dream editor, and his towering professional acumen is matched by his kindness, sense of humor, and joie de vivre. Ammi-Joan Paquette has been a model of serenity, an unerring copilot, and an impeccable source of smart answers to silly questions.

The Scholastic corporation is a hotbed of superpowers, including Emily Clement's eagle eye and quicksilver wit, Phil Falco's design prowess, and the entire production team's ferocious commitment to quality. Mike Maihack's pictorial wizardry brought my characters to exquisite, heroic life. Clap your hands and say "yeah" for the best agency-mates ever, the EMLA Gango! Thumbs up for the Society of Children's Book Writers and Illustrators, where I've made so many important connections and experienced so many pivotal moments.

Mega kudos to Kupkake Killa Martha Flynn and Demonslayer Ellen Oh, who are glitter-coated, two-fisted, superstar critique partners. Hallelujah for my cadre of beta readers: Bryan Bliss, Heather Burke, Elizabeth Harrin, Raynbow Gignilliat, Rose Green, Natalie Lorenzi, Nona Morrison, and Nancy Wagner lent me their eyes and brains (not literally, you ghoul). I'm grateful to Aimee Bender for all her encouragement, literary wisdom, and career perspective.

Verla Kay's Blueboards will always be my first true virtual home—Blueboarders represent!—and I'm also grateful for my wise and wacky friends at EMU's Debuts, the Enchanted Inkpot, the Mixed-Up Files of Middle-Grade Authors, and the Apocalypsies.

Finally, all my love goes to Miranda, Zoe, and Leo. They're the true source of everything meaningful in my life, and I'll always be the president of *their* fan club.

MIKE JUNG is an active blogger, parent, SCBWI member, and library professional. He lives in Oakland, California, with his wife and two young children. This is his first novel.

MIKE MAIHACK is a graduate of the Columbus College of Art and Design. He lives in Tampa, Florida. Find him online at www.cowshell.com.

This book was edited by Arthur A. Levine and designed by Phil Falco. The text was set in Adobe Garamond Pro, a typeface based on the roman types of Claude Garamond and the italic types of Robert Granjon. The display type was set in Futura, a typeface designed by Paul Renner between 1924 and 1926. The book was typeset by Christopher Grassi and printed and bound at R. R. Donnelley in Crawfordsville, Indiana. Production was supervised by Starr Baer, and manufacturing was supervised by Adam Cruz.